'TIS THE SEASON TO GUESS WHODUNIT....

The Baker Street rooming house was filled with a jolly group of lodgers. Too bad one of them was a killer. But which of the boarders had bats in the belfry instead of a partridge in a pear tree? Was it the lovely young Canadian whose tragic past included a "rest cure"...the perfect British major general whose taste for Gilbert and Sullivan might mask a hunger for violent death...the sinister landlady who planned a special Yuletide treat? Or was it one of the other Baker Street regulars: the very proper spinster with a strange secret...the Arab student with a blot on his copybook...the free-lance artist with an eye for the bizarre?

The solution to this unholy holiday case was all Scotland Yard wanted for Christmas. But if they couldn't unwrap the clues in time...come Christmas dinner, another hapless victim would be a cooked goose.

"A FAST-MOVING, ONE-SITTING TREAT."
—*Kirkus Reviews*

The
TWELVE
DEATHS
of
CHRISTMAS

Marian Babson

A DELL BOOK

Published by
Dell Publishing Co., Inc.
1 Dag Hammarskjold Plaza
New York, New York 10017

Dell® TM 681510, Dell Publishing Co., Inc.

ISBN: 0-440-19183-1

Reprinted by arrangement with Walker Publishing
Company, Inc.

Printed in the United States of America

Two Previous Dell Editions
December 1985
10 9 8 7 6 5 4 3

KRI

CHAPTER I

On the first day of Christmas . . .

It was a gratuitous insult on his part to introduce the subject of Broadmoor into what had hitherto been a perfectly amicable conversation.

At first, I could not believe that I had heard him aright. Failing that, I could not believe that he was serious.

But I had. And he was.

'You must understand you can't go on like this,' he said. 'Of course you understand it, you wouldn't have come to me otherwise. And that will count as a point in your favour with the police—'

'I came to consult you as my legal adviser about a slight problem,' I said stiffly. 'I see no need to bring the police into it.' I would not dignify his previous mention of Broadmoor by admitting that I had noticed it.

'No need!' He seemed to choke and gasped for breath. After a moment, he gave a weak smile and started again. 'Well, perhaps you could be right—' He did not meet my eyes. 'Why don't we have a drink and talk it over?'

He stretched out a hand to ring for his secretary, then grimaced nervously. 'I forgot,' he said. 'It's after hours. She'll have gone home long ago.' There was a trace of accusation in his tone. 'I was working late to try to get some things cleared up before the holiday.'

'I dropped in on impulse,' I agreed. 'I was just passing and hadn't really thought about the time. But you're right. I noticed it as I came through the outer office. Everyone else has gone home.'

'Well,' he said, 'we can still talk it over. Sit down again, please.'

'There is nothing to discuss.' I can tell when I am being humoured, and I resent it deeply. 'I should have known better than to expect help from such a source.'

'No, no,' he demurred. 'It's early days yet. You mustn't despair. We'll think of something.'

It has long been my contention that you cannot really trust *anyone*. This conversation was proving it. If you cannot trust and confide in your own legal adviser, who is supposed to have your own best interests at heart, then who else in the world can you—

'There's always an answer,' he went on, rather nervously, as though he were beginning to sense how deeply he had offended me. 'You mustn't despair.' It was the second time he had said that.

'I am not in despair,' I told him firmly. 'I see nothing to despair about. You have taken a small, basically unimportant, problem and blown it up out of all proportion. I can only assume you are doing so in order to justify the inflated fee note you will presently send to me.'

'Small!' He was choking again. 'Unimportant! Don't you see, the very fact that you can say that—'

He was repeating himself. I stopped listening. Really, he was being extremely boring. The thought crossed my mind that it might be as well to find myself a new legal adviser. I looked around the old-fashioned office. Someone more up to date. Someone who did not keep an enormous Victorian brass inkstand on his desk, one heavy glass well filled with red ink and the other with black ink, despite the fact that, in common with everyone else these days, he actually used a ballpoint pen. Someone who had a modern desk lamp, rather than an old green-shaded student's lamp with useless bits of candle-tending equipment dangling from it, despite the fact that it had been many years since he had been a student and the lamp had long since been wired for electricity.

'Right now, of course—' he bared his teeth in a false smile—'and I only mention it because we should consider the immediate alternative, the best option would appear to be Broadmoo—'

I picked up the long brass inkstand. He caught the movement out of the corner of his eye and, although his face had been a peculiar shade of grey since I had begun speaking, it turned even greyer.

'Wait a moment . . . Please . . .' He lifted a hand to protect the soft vulnerability of his temple. 'I didn't mean . . . Calm down. . . Surely we can discuss this like civili—'

I hadn't realized there was so much ink in the red inkwell. It mingled with the lesser trickle of the black, making curious patterns across the back of his sandy hair and the dull green of the desk blotter.

Honour was vindicated.

'And let that be a lesson to you!' I said, as I closed the office door behind me.

He didn't answer. Sheer pique, I should imagine, at having been worsted in our encounter.

Out in the street, darkness had already fallen. It

was, of course, fast approaching the shortest day of the year. How time flies!

I walked down the Strand towards Trafalgar Square and Whitehall to catch the bus back to my lodgings just off Baker Street. The darkness was compounded by the onset of a thin sleeting rain. The street lamps were strange pools of floating light above the heads of the pedestrians, casting weird shadows and turning every face into a grotesque mask of menace.

In the wider, deeper pool of light by Charing Cross Station, the black doom of newspaper hoardings proclaimed NEWSAGENT SLAIN IN SOHO, as did the headlines of the evening papers displayed by the newsvendors. How it upsets them when one of their own kind is involved.

I bought a paper to read later, thinking as I did so that perhaps it was as well that poor dear Mother had not survived into this Age of New Austerity to see what all our hopes and dreams had come to. Really, what a world we live in!

There were children in the bus queue and I smiled at them. I like children and get along well with them. Except for one or two unfortunate exceptions. But I mustn't think about them. It makes my head ache, and my head is aching quite enough already.

In fact, sometimes my head aches quite shockingly.

There was no bus in sight and, when one came, it would undoubtedly be full. For a moment I hesitated, and then the children began pushing each other and arguing, their shrill little voices cutting through me. My head gave a particularly nasty throb and that decided me. I hailed a taxi.

Sometimes, when my headache is particularly severe, I wonder whether or not I ought to consult a doctor about it.

But of course one can't trust doctors either . . .

CHAPTER II

Deck the halls with boughs of holly . . .

Iris Loring was at the top of the stepladder draping strands of tinsel over the crêpe paper streamers in the front hall when Anne Christopher arrived home. At the foot of the ladder, Mrs Daneson was doling out tinsel and instructions in roughly equal proportions.

'Over to the left more. No, not there. Be careful—that one's sliding—' She stooped and retrieved it from the floor, passing it back up to Iris.

'Filthy night.' She greeted Anne absently. 'Is it still sleeting?'

'Worse than ever.' Anne shook her umbrella, opened it again and set it down among the others in the corner of the hallway where they clustered like monster multicoloured toadstools. 'Thank heavens I don't have to go out again tonight.'

'I shouldn't imagine anyone would be going out again tonight.' Maude Daneson stepped back to survey Iris's handiwork. 'I think you need more in that corner, dear. Unless you were thinking of having balloons there? But I shouldn't advise it. Some of the lodgers are apt to come home a bit merry at this time of year and they seem to find balloons irresistible. It makes me very cross to be wakened by what sounds like gunshots in the early hours of the morning. So, no balloons.'

Anne collected her mail from the bulletin board and her newspaper from the hall table, shaking it out for a quick look at the front page. 'NEWSAGENT SLAIN IN SOHO . . . Discovered by early customer . . . an apparently motiveless killing . . .'

'Terrible, isn't it?' Maude Daneson looked over her shoulder. 'Someone ought to *do* something.'

'I'm sure the police are trying, Mrs Daneson,' Anne said, continuing to skim the paper for the gist of the story.

'I didn't mean *that*,' Mrs Daneson said. 'Everyone knows that the motiveless crimes are the hardest to solve—and sometimes they're never solved at all. I meant that it should *not* be left entirely to the police. Someone who'd do a thing like that—surely he's mad. Do you mean to say no one has noticed? He has to live among other people. He must be in contact with family, friends, acquaintances, people he works with—surely, *some*one must have noticed *some*thing suspicious. It's their duty to report him to the police—no matter how close the relationship.'

'It may not be that simple.' Iris spoke from the top of the ladder, where she had been taking advantage of Maude Daneson's inattention to redistribute the tinsel as she saw fit. 'He may be perfectly normal most of the time—unless something triggers him off. It no one ever triggered him off, they'd never know. To them, he'd just be that kindly man down the street who's always so good to his wife, adores his kiddies, climbs trees to rescue cats and helps little old ladies across the street.'

'This time he's killed a little old lady,' Anne said.

'And with her own scissors. A newsagent. Completely inoffensive. No enemies, no money taken from the till—but a top shelf of girlie magazines swept to the floor. The police think that may be some sort of clue.'

'Well, there you are.' Iris backed down the ladder. 'It's a sex maniac, a religious crank, a literary critic— or possibly just a member of the public who's fed up with constantly being faced with the sort of stuff that used to be sent in a plain brown wrapper to people who really wanted to look at it. That ought to narrow the field of suspects down to about ten million. Elementary, my—'

'I don't think you ought to laugh about it,' Maude Daneson said sharply. 'The woman is dead. In her own shop, going about her own business. It's dreadful! People aren't safe anywhere any more.'

'The police are appealing for witnesses—' Anne was still reading. 'Or anyone who might have noticed anything remotely suspicious—'

'The police!' Maude snorted. 'They made the same appeal about those two children they found in Regent's Park Lake last week—and what good did it do? No one ever notices anything, or admits it if they have. And at this time of the year, too! I don't know why things always seem worse at Christmas. Worse or better. But lately, it always seems to be worse instead of better. Perhaps that's what comes of growing old.'

'Shall I lock the door, Maude?' Iris asked.

'Yes, do. Anne is the last one in. If anyone wants to go out in this weather—well, they have their own keys. We certainly don't want to leave the front door open on a night like this, with a maniac roaming the West End.'

'Nonsense,' Iris said, snicking the lock home. 'He's

roaming well away from the Baker Street area, and there's no reason to suppose he's any more impervious to the weather than the rest of us. He's probably sitting in front of a roaring hearth this minute, roasting chestnuts for the children and planning what to serve the carol singers when they come round.'

'If he doesn't poison them,' Maude Daneson said darkly.

Leaving them to their amicable wrangling, Anne began to climb the stairs. She was half way up when she abruptly pulled her hand away from the banister. 'Oh!'

'What's the matter?' In the hall below, both Mrs Daneson's and Iris's faces turned upwards.

'There's ink all over my hand! It came off the banister just now. Wet black ink!'

'Oh dear. It didn't get on your coat, I hope?' Maude Daneson looked concerned.

'No.' Anne scrubbed at her hand with a paper handkerchief, and then scrubbed at the spot on the banister. 'No, it's all right. I think I've cleaned it off.'

'I suppose it's no more than one can expect with so many students in the house.' Mrs Daneson turned away, losing interest. 'But they ought to be more careful. I shall post a notice on the bulletin board to remind them.'

Despite the fact that she had watched Iris lock the front door, she went over and checked it.

'I *did* lock it, Maude,' Iris said.

'Yes, yes, I know. I just like to make sure.' Maude Daneson turned away from the door, beaming with relief. 'There,' she said. 'We're all locked in safe and cosy for the night now.'

CHAPTER III

On the second day of Christmas . . .

I don't know why that silly song should keep haunting me. I don't even like it. It never made any sense to me. When I was a child, I used to believe that the twelve days of Christmas were the days before Christmas itself. I had it mixed up with an Advent Calendar, I suppose, but it seemed to make sense that way. When I grew older and discovered that the counting started with Christmas Day, it seemed silly—and *foreign*, somehow. Not the way English people ought to count.

Even now, when I think of it . . . Although I seldom think of it. It's just that it seems to have crept into my mind lately and keeps circling around and around in there—it still seems as though it ought to be the days leading up to Christmas. These days. Another ten days until Christmas. And then I can relax.

A lot of people hate Christmas in England because all the shops are shut for three or four days in a row and no newspapers are published, but I rather like it. It takes away the burden of choice. When nothing is open, there is no reason for one to leave one's room. There is nowhere to go and no one will think it odd for anyone to stay in one's room with the door shut, just reading and resting.

I feel the need of rest lately. I don't know why. I have not been taking more exercise than usual, nor has my work load been any heavier.

Perhaps it has something to do with these headaches I've been having lately? After Christmas, I must really try to see a doctor. But we must get Christmas out of the way first. It will be good to have it over and done with.

But I shall be glad of the rest. I don't even mind there not being any postal service for several days. I don't get many letters anyway.

Mother used to get a lot of mail, especially at this time of the year. Letters, cards, and often presents, with every delivery. Sometimes it was hard to find space to display all the cards—every available surface was covered. How she loved that!

But the cards stopped coming after Mother died. They slowed to a trickle the first year or two, and then they stopped altogether, despite the fact that I always sent a card in return. I don't know why. I fear I lack the gift for friendship that Mother had. I'm socially stiff and awkward, I know. She always complained about that. Of course, many of the cards were from her contemporaries. I suppose they might have died, too.

No, I'm quite pleased that the postal service stops. Then no one can see how few cards I receive. Because they watch me in this house, I know they do. I catch them staring sometimes. They think they're clever about it and they smile and say, 'Good morning' or 'Good evening' when I meet their eyes. Quite as though that was all they had intended to do. And I answer pleasantly. I don't let them know that I know.

I do not think that I shall remain in this house

much longer. Perhaps, after Christmas, I shall seek
more congenial surroundings, find a place where the
people smile with their eyes as well as their lips and
do not watch, and watch . . . and wait. What are
they waiting for?

Yes, after Christmas.

There is so much I must do after Christmas.
Thinking about it all makes me tired. Perhaps that is
why I welcome the long holiday this year. When everything is closed and shuttered, one feels curiously
free, absolved from any necessity for action because
no effective action can be taken.

Yes, after Christmas.

Perhaps I ought to make a list. I must see a doctor,
look for new lodgings. And oh, yes, I wanted to see
my legal adviser—

But I seem to have forgotten for the moment why I
wanted to consult him.

My head! Oh no, no! I had thought I could get
through this day without a headache. Perhaps, if I
catch it in time . . . if I take some aspirins . . .
and lie down quietly . . .

Perhaps . . .

CHAPTER IV

I'm dreaming of a . . .

'Iris, be careful!' At the foot of the stairs, Patti James dodged back, trying to escape the flying white spray from the aerosol tin. 'What are you doing, anyway?'

'Sorry.' Iris took her finger off the button and lowered the tin. 'I haven't got this thing tamed yet. I'm *trying* to turn the hall mirror into an Olde Englishe mullioned window—can't you tell?'

'Oh yes.' Patti approached cautiously and peered at the clouded mirror. 'You're overdoing it a bit, aren't you? I mean, it would be nice if we could still see pieces of ourselves in it. We might want to check our make-up before we go out, or something.'

'That was what Miss Manning said. Well, more or less. She wanted to make sure her hat was on straight before she went out. Not that it would make any difference—with her.'

'Oh, she's not so bad,' Patti defended. 'Quite human, sometimes.' She began a cautious appraisal of the damage to her costume. 'You know, you've splattered that revolting stuff all over the hem of my coat.' She dabbed at it ineffectively. 'It *does* come off, doesn't it?'

'I hope so. I've managed to baptize everyone in the place with it this morning.'

'They must have been pleased.' Even Patti was beginning to sound irritated. 'Couldn't you have waited until we all left for the day before you started fooling around with that stuff? Where did you get it, anyway?'

'It was on sale at Selfridges'. There were masses of people buying it. It was a very popular item.'

'Popular with whom?' Patti continued scrubbing at her hem, with little apparent effect.

'I'm afraid you're just rubbing it in when you do that,' Iris said apologetically. 'Perhaps if you wait till it dries, you can scrape it off then.'

'Oh, Iris!' Patti let her annoyance explode.

'I know. I'm sorry,' Iris said. 'I couldn't know it would go all over the place like that. I think the nozzle leaks, or something. The one I really feel guilty about is Major Entwistle. It went all over his sleeve and I don't think he has much extra money for dry cleaning. He was awfully annoyed, and I couldn't blame him. I offered to try to sponge it off for him, but he just stamped out. I'll try again later—when he's cooled down a bit.'

'You can sponge my coat, too,' Patti said. 'If I can't get it off myself.'

'I will,' Iris said contritely. 'It's the least I can do. Perhaps I ought to put up a notice offering—'

'Now you're overdoing it,' Patti said.

'Well . . .' Iris brightened. 'I'll just offer to the ones who make any more of a fuss about it. I don't think some of them noticed at all and, with any luck, the stuff will wear off during the day.'

'I think you're being awfully optimistic,' Patti said. 'But I can't stand here talking all morning. I'm late for class now.'

'Bye-bye,' Iris said cheerily. 'Take care.'

'You're the one who'd better take care!' The door slammed behind Patti, a daunting reminder that she was still rather annoyed.

'I *wish* people wouldn't slam doors!' Maude Daneson emerged from her ground-floor flat. 'I think I shall have to put up a fresh notice about it. They're getting too careless again. Some people have no consideration for others at all.'

'You're so right, Maude,' Iris murmured, sliding the aerosol tin behind her back. But Maude appeared to have forgiven and forgotten the earlier unpleasantness. Apart from which, her hair gleamed from prolonged brushing which seemed to have worked, for no trace of the spray snow remained.

'Not that there's much room.' Maude frowned at the green baize-covered bulletin board, latticed with ribbons, which held the tenants' post. It was denuded at the moment, all the tenants having picked up their mail on the way out, but the afternoon delivery would crowd it out again, especially at this time of the year.

'I think the door just slipped out of her hand,' Iris said helpfully. 'I'm sure Patti didn't mean to slam it. It won't happen again.'

'Patti!' Maude Daneson rolled her eyes heavenwards. 'No, there's no point in writing out a new notice. I doubt that she'd bother to read it, and she'd certainly never think that it was intended for her, if she did. These Canadians!'

The comment was perfunctory and Iris did not bother to answer. Besides, Maude had a look in her eye which portended a change of subject. Iris braced herself warily but fondly. She was prepared to put up

with any number of Maude's foibles out of sheer
gratitude.

When she had descended from the North, fresh
from Art School and prepared to battle her way as a
freelance through the London jungle, she had been
armed only with Maude's address and the assurances
of older members of the family that a tenuous kinship existed—cousins, an unspecified number of times
removed.

Maude, however, had welcomed her with open
arms and a scheming glint in her eyes, subsequently
explained by the knowledge that a procession of au
pairs had decamped abruptly and Maude was desperate for a resident housekeeper she could depend
upon. Kinship worked both ways.

Once Iris had seen the basement flat which went
with the job, complete with french windows opening
on to a generous garden and flooded with glorious
light during most of the daylight hours, both their
problems had been solved. The work was not ardu-
ous—a daily help came in to make the beds and clean
the rooms—and Iris had plenty of time for her own
work.

The arrangement had worked better than either of
them had had a right to expect and they had existed
in a state of amiable symbiosis ever since. Maude
saved the pocket money demanded by an au pair and
Iris lived rentfree at a better address than she could
otherwise have afforded. Even now that Iris was becoming known, even sought after, in her own field of
illustration, neither of them felt like changing such a
mutually satisfactory arrangement.

'I suppose we must make allowances for Patti,'
Maude sighed. 'Poor child, so far away from home. She

isn't flying back for Christmas, is she?'

'It's a long way to go for just a few days,' Iris said. 'And expensive. Besides, I think she's rather looking forward to an old-fashioned Christmas in England.'

'Yes,' Maude went on. 'We have quite a few students here who won't be able to get home for Christmas. Poor dears. Not to mention some of our older lodgers. I haven't heard that Major Entwistle is going anywhere, either, have you? I suspect he has nowhere to go. He served out of this country for so long. When he returned, he found his old friends had scattered and it's hard to start all over again, especially for a man alone. It happened to a lot of old soldiers.' Maude sighed. 'The price of Empire—and for what? That, too, has scattered to the four winds.'

'From bits of gossip I've heard going around,' Iris contributed, 'I'd say we were going to have quite a full house over Christmas. A good dozen, at least.'

'Just as I suspected!' Maude nodded her head in satisfaction. 'Which is why I've been thinking I ought to do something about the situation.'

'Oh?' Iris was wary. Experience had taught her that Maude's *I's* invariably meant *'we'* and often boiled down to *'you'*.

'We cannot have them sitting alone in their rooms on Christmas Day,' Maude declared. 'It wouldn't be *right*.'

'I don't think they mind,' Iris said. 'I mean, if they minded, they'd do something about it, wouldn't they?'

'Do what?' Maude asked. 'Try to cook a piece of chicken over the little gas-ring in their rooms? Or go out to some expensive hotel or restaurant for a meal that will cost too much and not be worth it? And then, they'd still be alone.'

'Perhaps they want to be alone,' Iris said, but it was the last throw of dice loaded against her. 'They might prefer it.'

'No!' Maude shook her head decisively. 'I cannot allow that on Christmas Day. Not to people I like to think of as guests under my roof. Not when I have a full-sized kitchen and cooker and a large dining-room table. I can seat a dozen easily. I shall invite everyone to my flat and *we* shall serve them Christmas dinner.'

'I thought you were going away to your nephew's for Christmas,' Iris said, a dim memory surfacing.

'They telephoned last night.' Maude looked only slightly abashed. 'The children have come down with mumps. I *couldn't* go and risk passing mumps on to our guests here. Apart from which, I've never had them myself. It will be far better for me to stay home and entertain here this year.'

'I see,' Iris said, everything suddenly becoming clear. Especially Maude's sudden concern for the welfare of her lodgers—which had not bothered her at all last year.

'Well . . .' Maude drew on her gloves. 'I must rush and do some shopping now. I haven't nearly enough on hand for Christmas dinner for all of us. It's going to take a lot of organization. I'll do some preliminary shopping now and then, when I come back, I can make out a shopping list and perhaps you can go out later this afternoon.'

Iris realized that she should have known that was coming. 'I could come with you now, Maude,' she suggested. 'And carry your shopping for you.' A pack-horse, after all, was what Maude required and it made no difference to her personally whether she went out now or later.

'No—' Maude shook her head fretfully. 'I'm not going straight to the shops. I want to walk around for a bit first—I feel I need some fresh air. I'm afraid I'm not up to any more conversation, either.'

'All right,' Iris said. 'It was just a thought.'

'You *do* understand, don't you?' At the door, Maude hesitated, obviously fearing that she had given offence. 'I really *must* be alone. Actually—' she brushed a hand across her brow—'I have one of my heads—'

'Do you want some aspirin?' Iris was instantly solicitous.

'I've taken some. I just want some fresh air now.' Maude smiled wanly. 'I'll be all right soon.'

CHAPTER V

On the third day of Christmas . . .

That filthy, beastly stuff! It's everywhere! One can't get away from it. Even here in the chemist's. And that salesgirl—little slut! She's supposed to be serving the customers, not playing around with that terrible aerosol spray. Look at her—paying no attention. *Deliberately* paying no attention. When she can see that I've been standing here, waiting. Perhaps, if I clear my throat . . .

No use. She has no intention of bothering with customers. That's the trouble with England today. No one cares. No one gives any service. Take the salary and do as little as possible for it. No question of *earning* it. That doesn't enter into their calculations. Selfish and petty-minded. Only interested in themselves and their little fads of the moment.

Such a ghastly fad, this one. Artificial snow. Sprayed-on. What do they see in it? And yet, it seems to be everywhere. You can see it on nearly every window—and mirror.

There—she's finishing the tin. Perhaps now . . .

No. She's just tossed the empty tin into the waste basket, reached under the counter and brought out another, and begun spraying more of the stuff on the window. If she puts much more on, passers-by won't be able to see the goods on display at all. Perhaps that's her idea. The ultimate in customer deterrence. If they can't see what's on sale, they can't come in and bother her. She can spend her days undisturbed.

'Miss!' I don't care, I'm going to disturb her. I must. I must get something for this headache. Aspirins don't seem strong enough any more. Perhaps some powders . . .

'Miss! I've been waiting for ten minutes! If you haven't the time to serve me yourself, perhaps you might be good enough to call the Manager.'

'He isn't here.' The girl barely turned, looking thoroughly bored.

'I might have known it. I dare say you don't carry on like this when someone in authority is present. In that case, perhaps I ought to come back later and have a word with him.'

'You've never been here ten minutes!' That made her turn her head. 'You've only just come in the shop. I can't drop everything and wait on you. Doing the displays is part of my job, too.'

In her agitation, she kept her finger on the button of the spray tin. The window was now completely obscured. One could barely discern people passing like shadows on the other side of the glass.

It would be a nasty job to clean all that off and start again. It served her right. Perhaps I smiled, for she swivelled suddenly to see what I was looking at.

'*Now* look what you've made me do!'

Really, these creatures are frightfully bad-tempered. If she had been attending to her job properly, it would never have happened. Before I could say as much, she turned on *me*.

'Oh!' The filthy, beastly stuff—all over my sleeve. The second time in two days. 'You did that deliberately!'

'And you can tell that to the Manager, too!' She came out from behind the counter, advancing on me, deliberately *aiming* the nozzle at my face.

I backed away a step or two. I shouldn't have. It was an instinctive reaction. She thought she had me on the run. Retreating. Never! I stopped and stood my ground. She continued to advance. Thank heavens there was no one else in the shop. One doesn't wish to make a scene, but she was leaving me no option.

'Don't you dare!' I thundered.

'Dare?' She gave a short ugly laugh. 'Don't *you* give *me* orders! Who do you think you are? I'll show you—'

I caught her arm in self-defence and tried to push her away. We struggled awkwardly for a moment, but I was stronger. Breeding tells. Then, quite fittingly, she slipped on some of that filthy stuff she had spilled on the floor. It hadn't dried and was quite slippery, it seemed.

She went down heavily, striking her head against the counter. It served her right. She lay motionless. The tin of spray snow rolled away from her outflung hand and came to rest against my foot.

She ought to be taught a lesson! I found that I was shaking with rage. She had intended to spray that stuff in my face—I had read the intention in her beady glittering little eyes. *An eye for an eye, and a tooth for a tooth!* Even the Bible said that.

I stooped and picked up the tin. As I did so, she moaned faintly. She would be coming round in a minute. Her horrid red-rimmed little mouth was open and I knew the vile words that would be issuing from it with returning consciousness. Her mouth ought to be washed out with soap!

In every way, she needed a lesson. I didn't have any soap, but I had the tin of spray snow. And I still had my headache, growing worse by the second, with a roaring in my ears.

And that was her fault, too! If she'd waited on me, given me something I could have taken—

But they think only of themselves. Perhaps *her* head never bothered her. Perhaps *she* never knew what it was to have a throbbing, splitting, endless pain tearing her mind apart. Perhaps *that* was what she ought to learn!

I stooped again, thrusting the nozzle of the spray tin into her open mouth. As her eyelids began to twitch, I pushed hard on the spray button. The stuff hissed as it rushed into her mouth. I kept my finger on the button. It was a fresh tin, barely used. There was enough to teach her a good lesson.

She choked, retched, tried to force herself back to consciousness, tried to raise her head . . .

I pushed her back. When she woke up, I wanted the job to be done. I wanted her to know what it felt like.

After a moment, she ceased to struggle. Her mouth seemed to be full, the snow was beginning to ooze out of the corners. She looked as though she were foaming at the mouth.

There still seemed to be plenty of artificial snow in the tin. For good measure, I pushed the nozzle up each nostril in turn and gave a good long squirt.

Now she looked as though her nose was running, too. Running foam, running snow.

I couldn't help laughing. I became aware that I was feeling better. The roaring in my ears was receding, the pain in my head seemed to be lessening. Perhaps I wouldn't need those powders, after all.

It was just as well. I doubted that she would be willing to get them for me when she recovered consciousness. These people hate to be bested! I must find another shop.

At the door, I paused and turned back. 'Let that be a lesson to you,' I told her.

She lay there motionless. She wouldn't answer.

Sulky bitch!

CHAPTER VI

Christmas is coming, the goose hangs fat . . .

The stiff white envelopes were slotted into the latticed ribbons of the bulletin board in the front hall. Envelopes with a charity Christmas seal in the upper right-hand corner rather than a stamp. They loomed ominously behind the smaller, less substantial envelopes that had arrived in the regular post and were tucked in front of them.

Iris hovered at the end of the hallway, vaguely feeling that it was part of her unofficial duty to soften the blow to the unwary. Maude did not realize how overpowering she could sometimes be. Nor, to give her credit, did she have any idea of how fraught the landlord-tenant relationship could often be.

At four-thirty the first of the tenants returned. Iris waited cautiously in the shadows until she could see which one it was. Patti. That was all right. She came forward casually, as though she just happened to be passing.

'Hi!' Patti greeted her cheerfully, reaching eagerly for the cluster of brightly-coloured envelopes in her section of the lattice. She shuffled through them happily, identifying friends by the handwriting and postmarks. Until she came to the last one, the stiff formal white one. She inspected it with foreboding and raised anxious eyes to Iris. 'What's up?'

'Nothing to worry about,' Iris assured her quickly. 'It's just that Maude's in one of her Lady Bountiful moods. "Oh, come, all ye peasants". That is,' she clarified, 'Maude is inviting all the tenants to Christmas festivities in her flat on the Day. Turkey and all the trimmings, Christmas crackers and paper hats, plum pudding and brandy sauce. And probably charades, too—if you can bear it.'

'Well, great!' Patti turned the invitation over dubiously, not opening it. 'Except—'

'Except what?' Iris found that she was prepared to be as fiercely protective of Maude as of the tenants. Maude had made up her mind to a party to brighten their lives—and it would be unfair to cheat her of it.

'Well, I'm not going to be alone over the holiday. Pammi, my sister, is flying over to spend Christmas with me. We wanted to be together and she's started working and has a good salary, so it's easier for her to come over here than for me to go back over there.

'Besides—' Patti looked away, carefully controlling her voice and expression—'it's our first real Christmas without our parents. They died in a car crash a month before Christmas last year, and then I was quite ill for a long time. In fact, I don't remember Christmas or New Year last year. So we decided we wanted to be in different surroundings this year. To spend Christmas in a place that didn't hold any memories for us—'

'I'm sure you're wise,' Iris said hastily, as Patti's voice threatened to break. 'And I'm *positive* Maude would love to have you both come.'

'That *would* be nice,' Patti said wistfully. 'We'd thought of having Christmas dinner at Pammi's hotel, but it would be much nicer here with friends around us. If you're *sure* Maude wouldn't mind—?'

'Maude will be delighted,' Iris said firmly, sure of her ground. 'She's planning for a big party and not all the tenants will be able to come. Some of them—' Iris gestured towards the bulletin board—'will have their own plans, and others will be going to relatives for the holiday.'

'I suppose they will.' Patti looked more cheerful. 'Well, if you're sure—'

'I'll be depending on you to help us with the festivities,' Iris said. 'It's going to be a bit more complicated than I think Maude realizes. I mean, have you thought that not all of us are going to be celebrating the same thing?'

'That's right.' Patti was caught by the idea. 'Mr Stein will really be celebrating Hanukkah, won't he?'

'And Ahmed will be celebrating Ramadan, probably. And—' Iris spread her hands despairingly—'what on earth do you imagine Major Entwistle will be celebrating?'

'The Winter Solstice, perhaps.' Patti laughed merrily. 'Okay, Pammi and I will try to take some of the heat off you if things begin to get sticky. Perhaps Anne can help, too.'

'Anne may just be part of the problem herself,' Iris said. 'Her boy-friend is moving in with her for the holidays. I haven't quite dared to mention it to Maude yet. I'm not sure what she'll think about it. She may decide to be modern and shrug it off, or she may go all old-fashioned and get upset about it.'

'Do you think she would?' Patti frowned with concern. 'Oh, I hope not. I—I always think of this as such a *happy* house. I wouldn't want anything to happen to spoil it. I keep telling Pammi how lucky I was to find a place like this.'

'It *is* a good place,' Iris agreed, thinking of some of the places she might have ended up—places some of her friends occupied. 'And I don't *really* think Maude will mind. Not *too* much. It's just a question of picking the right time and the right way to break it to her.'

'If I can be of any help—?'

'No, I don't think so, thanks.' Her brain working quickly, Iris decided that, if she could lump Patti's sister in with Anne's boy-friend and discuss the problem of two extra guests, they might both be made to sound equally innocent. It was worth a try, at least. Or was she making a mountain out of a molehill in fearing that Maude would mind at all? Maude's wartime generation, although more discreet, had hardly been more innocent.

'I don't *think* Maude will make a thing of it,' she said, encouraging herself as much as Patti. 'In any case, it's nothing to do with you and your sister. Maude will love to have you both, I *know* that.'

'Well, we'll do all we can to help out,' Patti promised. 'If you want anything, just let us know. And look, suppose we bring something along as our contribution to the party? What do you think—wine, chocolates, fruit?'

'I think everyone is going to say that,' Iris answered honestly. 'Why don't we wait a while until we see what's on offer from the others? Otherwise, we're going to wind up awash with sherry or tangerines and short on something else we ought to have. Would you mind waiting a bit for the answer?'

'Of course not,' Patti said. 'Just let me know in

time to get to the shops before they shut. And—' her eyes were suddenly over-bright and sparkling—'and thanks. And thank Maude for me. It—it's so sweet of her—'

The latch rasped in the front door and Patti turned and fled up the stairs before anyone else could see how perilously close to tears she had come.

CHAPTER VII

God rest ye merry, gentlemen,
Let nothing you dismay . . .

'You know what this means, don't you?' Detective-Superintendent Knowles asked his team mates accusingly.

They looked back at him uncomfortably, groping for the right answer. Or rather, trying not to admit that answer—even to themselves.

'There was no sign of sexual assault,' one of them said, obviously trying to look on the bright side. 'The pathologist will have to confirm, of course. But it doesn't look like that sort of case.'

'Thanks for nothing,' Knowles said bitterly. The information seemed to sink him deeper in gloom. He had already known that.

'Nothing seems to be missing,' another of them contributed. 'The till hasn't been touched and the drugs cupboard seems intact. The chemist will have to check his inventory, of course, to make sure. Later. He's under sedation right now. She was his niece. Fifteen, and her first job during school holidays. Her parents thought it would be nicer for her to work for one of the family her first time out. So that he could show her the ropes and . . . sort of . . . look after her . . .' The voice trailed away into silence.

They had all seen her. They had seen a lot in the course of duty in the West End, but they had never seen anything like that before. They never wanted to again.

'Whoever did it was crazy!' Detective-Sergeant Preston blurted out. 'Only a maniac could have done something like that.'

'Precisely.' Knowles nodded. 'And it's the *same* maniac—I'll bet on it.' He paused, but no one took him up on the offer.

'The kids in the Regent's Park Lake, the woman at the newsagent's in Upper Soho, the solicitor in Middle Temple—I had hopes our villain was moving away when that one came in. But now this.' Knowles shook his head.

They knew what he meant. In dealing with a series of crimes perpetrated by the same person, the jurisdiction went to the manor in which the original crime had taken place. Those small bodies lifted out of Regent's Park Lake had marked the beginning of this current bizarre series, which meant that the case devolved on them. The newsagent had been just over the border into their territory, as well. The City of London police would cheerfully hand over the Middle Temple murder to them, as would any other district with reason to believe that the same killer had been at work. Rather as though some carelessly misplaced belonging had turned up in their area: 'Yours, I believe.' Not that any other manor could be blamed for that; everyone had too much of their own work to do in these days of rising crime rate. They, too, would have happily handed over to anyone who wanted to claim this lot, but they couldn't because it was theirs. They knew it.

'He's ours!' Knowles voiced the common thought. 'All these savage, motiveless attacks on innocent citizens. He's operating mainly in our manor, chances are he lives in our manor. Somewhere—'

They were silent, thinking of the extent of their manor. It ranged from the expensive hotels, to the exclusive apartment blocks around Regent's Park, to the bed-and-breakfast houses which weren't quite grand enough to be labelled hotels, not to mention the hot pillow havens at the sleazier end of the tourist trade. There were too many bedsitting houses and company hostels, which, together with the hotels, took in a sizeable proportion of the floating population, young and old, lost, lonely, eccentric—and now, mad.

Preston was still lost in his own thoughts. He had given the right answer by accident. *Accident.* When he'd left home this morning, the kids had been playing with two tins of spray snow, just like—He wondered how soon he could get to a telephone and call his wife, tell her to take those tins away from the kids. They were dangerous—

'If we can't wrap this up by Christmas,' Knowles went on, 'it means *we* won't have a Christmas. All leave will be cancelled, we'll be on duty over the holiday. No nice turkey dinner with the family. We'll be eating in the canteen—if we're lucky—'

A vision of the dead girl rose up in Prestons' mind, her mouth filled with the congealed snow, her nostrils clogged. The force of the compressed gas must have driven the soft substance deep into her lungs and into the sinus cavities around her eyes and nose and ears, filling them, hardening in them—He shook his head, trying to clear the image from his mind. His stomach quaked perilously.

'I'm not hungry,' he said. There was a murmur of agreement.

'I suppose—' the voice was tentative and soft, as though not wishing to draw attention to itself. 'I suppose we'll have to check out the uncle—and the aunt—just to make sure.'

'Naturally.' Knowles sighed wearily. 'But they'll be in the clear. I'll guarantee it. This is another one in the series—and there *is* a series building up. We've got to stop it as fast as we can. The media aren't on to it yet, but when they hear about this one—'

This one. The nastiest of the lot. So far.

'You know what's happened, don't you?' Knowles faced his men. 'It's a nightmare come true. A homicidal maniac stumbling on the formula for the perfect murder: kill a stranger. Someone you have no connection with; someone who can't be traced back to you.

'And the method varies every time. There *is* no method. No nice neat *modus operandi* that can be fed into a computer. This villain is a spur-of-the-moment operator, using whatever means comes to hand. Turning the most innocent-seeming objects into deadly weapons. Putting normal everyday items to a use no normal mind could conceive—'

Preston fought down the memory of those spray snow canisters in the tiny hands of his offspring. Perhaps he shouldn't phone his wife and have her confiscate them. Perhaps it might be wiser to wait—if he could—until the kids went to bed tonight and then throw the things away and tell the kids they'd been used up. Let the kids have one of their Christmas presents early to distract them—the paint set, perhaps, or the building set. They ought to be harmless enough. He had a brief agonizing vision of the pointed handle of a paintbrush being jabbed into a childish eye, of the small blocks of a building set being jammed into a childish throat or up a tiny nose. Nothing in the world was completely harmless. Everything could be turned to lethal use by a distorted mind bent on destruction.

Preston shuddered, suddenly aware that this case would change them all, was changing him already. Part of his innocence—an innocence he had not known he still possessed—was slipping away, never to be regained. People were so fragile, so much at the mercy of those surrounding them. Let one mind snap apart and uncounted numbers were unknowingly at risk, never suspecting that some unthinking grimace, some unconscious gesture, might be interpreted as a hostile threat by an unbalanced observer and met accordingly.

'He's in *our* manor—' Knowles was saying much the same thing. 'Walking around, probably looking just the same as anyone else. Except that he's a homicidal maniac with a hair-trigger temper—and no one knows what's likely to set him off. We've got to find him before he strikes again.'

CHAPTER VIII

On the fourth day of Christmas . . .

How I hate the rush hour! The crowds. The pushing and shoving. The total lack of consideration for others. And it's worse at this time of year. You'd think people would time their Christmas shopping so that they didn't get caught up in the rush hour. For their own sakes, even though they obviously care about no one else.

But no. They won't. So everything is made twice as bad by these obnoxious creatures from the suburbs cluttering up the underground with their carrier bags and shopping baskets and nasty whining overtired brats in tow. Stupid, inconsiderate—and absolutely vicious, the way they push other people out of their path. As though they had more rights than the regular commuters who travel this way all year round.

Like that poor man in the corner, jammed up against the door by that frightful woman with the pink Christmas tree sticking out of her carrier bag and that ghastly child ready to burst out crying any minute. I've seen that man before, a pleasant chap in the ordinary way, but now his face is a most unhealthy colour and he looks as though he might have a heart attack momentarily. Either that, or he'll fall out of the train and be trampled as soon as the door is opened. By rights, he ought to have a seat, but they're all filled with women and children who should have done their shopping in the morning and been at home now—out of everyone's way. But they don't care. They don't think of other people at all.

I wish I hadn't come this way tonight. I hate having to change at Oxford Circus. It's like a cattle pen. I should have taken the bus. But they're no better at this time of year. The queues are abominable and the women with carrier bags even more inescapable when they're crowding into a seat beside you with their shopping taking up as much space as they do, leaving you no room to breathe, even.

I wish Christmas were over. Although things don't improve very much then, with all the Sales starting. It's the forced jollity I can't stand. They knock you across the back of the legs with their shopping carts, or nearly poke your eye out with something long-handled and awkward they're carrying, and then they expect you to laugh and forgive them just because it's Christmas time.

I'll feel better when Christmas is over. It's the nervous strain that gets me down. Too many people all trying to be in the same place at the same time. That, and—I must be honest—remembering other, happier Christmases. But Mother is gone now. Shall I ever grow accustomed to that fact? She wouldn't want me to be unhappy, but I can't help it.

New scenes, new faces, New Year. Yes, that will help. But first, there are the remains of this old year to be got through. Somehow.

Oh! Right in the small of my back! And not even an apology! I turned and glared at her, but she looked right through me, trying to pretend innocence. Quite as though that fishing rod sticking out of her bag belonged to someone else. The sheer brazen effrontery of her! *And* that brat of hers!

And now the train is stopping in this hot airless tunnel just outside the station. Why must they always do that? Why can't the authorities arrange things better?

I must be calm. I can't be the only one in this carriage who feels a touch of claustrophobia. I mustn't be the one who cracks up. I won't be!

But my head is beginning to throb again. I should have walked home, stayed out in the open air. I'd have been all right then.

That's better. We're moving again. Sliding into the station. I'll get away from these frightful people then. Unfortunately, I'll probably pick up another lot just as bad. They must crawl out from under stones this time of year! Look at the crowds of them lining the platform, packed solid all the way back to the wall. It's a wonder the ones at the back don't push the ones in front right off the platform into the path of the incoming trains. Especially now, when so many of them have awkward bundles and may not realize how they're knocking other people about. Nasty accidents can happen that way.

Ow! It's a pity an accident can't happen to that beastly woman behind me! Unfortunately, she's more the type likely to cause one. Why can't she watch what she's doing?

And that other child *is* going to cry. What a penetrating voice it has. Nearly as penetrating as its mother's. Why do these women have to scream at their children? It only aggravates the situation and makes bystanders twice as uncomfortable.

Those voices are going right through my head. *Oh, my head!* I can't stand this another moment. Why don't they open those doors? What are they waiting for?

Ah, that's better. Oh, I knew it! That poor man by the door nearly fell. Not that he actually could—the people are packed in too tightly. There's only one way to fall in a tube station during rush hour. It's a pity more of them don't.

Well, wait until we get off, can't you? Why do they always try to push aboard without letting anyone off? Can't they realize there'll be more room for them if they let the others off first? It must be some sort of lemming-like hysteria that takes control of them. They hardly even *look* human, pushing and shoving, terrified that someone else might occupy six inches of space they want for themselves. Animals!

Out at last—but with that fishing rod poking into my back all the way. I shall be black and blue tonight. Why couldn't she have stayed on the train? Oh no—she's coming my way, switching over to the Bakerloo line, too! Shall I never escape her? And now *her* brat has started crying—and *her* scolding voice is just as sharp and painful to the ears as the voice we've left behind. I don't think I can stand it much longer.

How their voices rebound from the curved walls of the tunnel. Even with all the other people around, that sharp scolding voice and the high-pitched howling bounce back to hurt one's ears. If only I could get farther ahead of them, but there are so many people crowded shoulder to shoulder and all surging in the same direction. There's no chance of getting through.

Damn! That fishing rod again! It's unbearable—it really is! They're terrible people. Why is the world so full of terrible people? No one would miss them if they all went away. Even the man the fishing rod must be destined for would surely be better off without *her* around his neck. He could go away and fish in peace then. Maybe that's why he goes fishing now—to get away from her and that brat for some peace and quiet. I wouldn't be surprised. I begin to feel that I'd do anything to get away from them myself.

My head won't stop throbbing. Every shriek of that child—every complaint of that woman—goes right through it. No consideration—you'd think they were the only people in the world, the way they carry on.

This tunnel is endless—I've always hated it. And someone's been sick over there. How nauseating! Perhaps if I can just hold my breath until I'm well past—

But that makes my head worse. I feel quite dizzy. I must, *must* breathe—

Why can't they shut up? Why can't she stop poking that thing into me? I should never have come this way. Perhaps I ought to go upstairs right now and take a bus the rest of the way.

Ah, that's better—but not much. The end of the tunnel at last, but this platform is as crowded as the one we've just left. Still, we can spread out a little more. I can get away from that awful fishing rod—

There, just a short sidestep and *she's* ahead of *me* now. Now it's my turn to do the pushing—Let *her* get out of *my* way—

Strange, how the wind rushes along the tunnel just ahead of the incoming train. It's a much more reliable source of information than the indicator board as to when a train is actually coming. Stale, dry air, but cool on one's face and faintly refreshing nevertheless.

So many people, milling about on the platform, no one paying the least attention to anyone else. Except to jostle them out of the way. That frightful woman has pushed her way to the very edge of the platform now. She has her uses, though, I've let her clear the path through the others and I'm right behind her.

But that means I'll be in the same carriage with her again. No, I don't like that idea. If only my head were clearer, I'd have been able to follow that thought through earlier. No, I can't stand that—

First, the rush of wind on your face, then the roaring sound of the train, coming closer . . . closer . . . While, all around, people inch nearer and nearer to the edge of the platform . . .

OH! How terrible, how awful! I always thought something like that would happen some day. But she let go of the child's hand before she tumbled over. That's rather a pity.

My head! The screaming! The screech of brakes! Too late, of course. There was too much momentum for the train to stop in time. But the noise, the panic, the uproar!

That settles it. I shall definitely go upstairs and take the bus. The service will be shut down here for hours while they sort out this mess. And just look at the way people have crowded up to try to see what's going on—except for the ones who are trying to comfort the little boy. No, it's time to slip away quietly and not get involved.

I always said there'd be a nasty accident some day.

CHAPTER IX

The door is always open, the neighbours come to call ...

The tenants were late tonight. Iris loitered near the top of the basement stairs, ready to dodge back if Maude should see her, equally ready to dart forward for an impromptu conference with the tenants as they came in. But it was past time for the first of them to arrive—way past time. By now, the last of them should be getting in, and the first still had not arrived yet.

Something must be wrong somewhere.

Immediately she shook herself mentally, repudiating the thought. Why should anything be wrong? The stores were open late tonight, Christmas was drawing closer by the hour, naturally people would be doing last-minute shopping. Even the tenants had to do their shopping sometime.

It was because of some increasing sense of unease that seemed to be in the air. There was no sense to it. Nothing could possibly have happened to the tenants—not to *all* of them in one fell swoop—they were too scattered, working or studying in areas many miles apart. Of course they were all right. Of course they must simply be delayed by . . . *by a sudden*

spontaneous desire to do their Christmas shopping,
striking each one of them on this particular evening?

Iris moved forward uneasily, advancing on the
front door as though to take it by surprise. She felt
foolish, but could not resist the impulse to open the
door and look up and down the street to see if any of
them were coming yet.

They weren't. The whole street was, in fact, curiously deserted, given the time of day. Usually, at this
hour, the street was alive with homecoming residents
hurrying towards the warmth and light of their re-
spective lodgings.

Iris felt her sense of unease increase. Something
was wrong—somewhere.

She stepped back into the hallway, shutting the
door behind her, and turned to face—Maude.

'You're worried, too,' Maude said. 'Where *is* everyone tonight?'

'Something must be wrong—' Iris voiced her
thought for the first time. 'There must be a hold-up
somewhere along the line.'

'I got home not half an hour ago,' Maude said. 'Everything was all right *then*.'

'It takes time for these things to build up,' Iris said.
'Something could have been going wrong at just
about that time.'

Maude frowned. 'Let's turn on the News.' Maude
beckoned her into the ground-floor flat. 'Perhaps
they'll have something about it.'

'It takes time for things to show up on the News,
too.' Nevertheless, Iris followed her into the flat. She
noticed that Maude left the door ajar so that they
could hear anyone arriving home.

The screen glowed, flickered, and lurched into life,

catching a commentator mid-sentence, looking awkward and abrupt thus wrenched out of context. He finished a meaningless bulletin and proceeded, with a firming of voice and image, into another bulletin which concerned an event of minimal interest occurring on the other side of the world. That disposed of, he continued to bore his way through several other uninteresting items.

'You were right.' Maude switched off the set. 'If anything *has* happened, there obviously hasn't been time for the news to catch up with it.'

'Try the radio,' Iris suggested. 'They can give more up-to-the-minute information, they don't have to worry about what they look like while they're reading the latest flash. And they specialize in telling about traffic snarl-ups, burst water mains, and . . . that sort of thing . . .' she finished limply, aware that neither she nor Maude believed that anything so innocuous might have delayed the tenants.

Without a word, Maude snapped on the radio, betraying that she too was a victim of the increasing unease spreading throughout the city.

But there was nothing untoward being reported over the radio, either.

'Of course,' Iris murmured, no longer wondering where the thought came from. 'They have to wait until they've notified the next-of-kin first, don't they?'

'I don't like this year!' Maude shuddered into non-sequitur. 'Suddenly it all seems to be going wrong. I'll be glad when it's over.'

'That won't be long now,' Iris comforted. 'Just a couple more weeks—'

They both heard the sharp click of the front latch at the same time. They hurtled forward, colliding in the doorway, and emerged into the front hall in time to see Eva Manning closing the door behind her.

'*Too* awful—' Miss Manning said faintly. She did not seem to find their attitudes surprising, rather it seemed as though she had been expecting them there to lend needed comfort and support.

'*Too* frightful—' She stretched out one hand, appealing to them. 'Really, people *are* incredible. Imagine committing suicide in Oxford Circus tube station at the height of rush hour traffic. And at Christmas, too! People are so inconsiderate—There ought to be a law against it—'

'So *that's* what happened!' Maude exclaimed. 'But I came through Oxford Circus myself about an hour ago. Nothing had happened then.'

'In front of a train . . .' Eva Manning raised her hand before her eyes, as though warding off a vision. 'I . . . I didn't go and *look* . . . I heard them talking about it . . . heard the screams . . . they said she . . . she simply *leaped* in front of a train . . .'

'Come in and have a drink.' Maude was on one side of Eva Manning, signalling Iris with an indication of the head to take the other arm. Together, they supported her into Maude's flat and Maude poured a generous dollop of brandy and thrust it into her unresisting hand.

The front latch clicked again and Iris darted into the front hall to see Anne Christopher, white and shaken, leaning against the front door as though, having managed to close it, she lacked the strength to do anything else.

'You, too?' Iris motioned her forward. 'Come on. First Aid is being served in here.'

Maude took one look at Anne's face and poured another glass of brandy.

'Leave the door open,' she instructed Iris. 'There are obviously going to be more of them. I think practically everyone in the house comes through Oxford Circus station.' She measured the level of brandy with a thoughtful gaze. 'Perhaps you wouldn't mind popping round to the Off-Licence—'

The front door slammed emphatically. Before either Iris or Maude could get there, Patti appeared in the doorway.

'It's wild!' she declared. 'I've never seen anything like it! Dickens never told us the half of it. This is the first time in my life I've seen policemen standing out in the middle of the street with loudspeakers directing the pedestrian traffic on the *sidewalk!* It's your genuine old-fashioned Olde Englishe Christmas Shopping. Pammi is never going to believe it!'

Maude automatically poured another glass of brandy although Patti seemed in a state of euphoria beyond any need for it.

'Thanks.' Patti took it and advanced into the room, still expounding on her theme. 'And *try* and fight your way round Selfridges' corner—I thought I'd never get past! Where do they all come from?' Patti took a swallow of her drink and continued.

'Honestly, for the first time, I've got a certain amount of sympathy for nuts who go around murdering everybody. The more the population is cut down, the better. By the time I was half way around that corner, if I'd had a machine-gun—' She braced an imaginary gun, aimed it, swivelled it slowly, and, 'Brrr-rrah-ah-ah-ah—'

'Patti, dear, please . . .' Maude said weakly.

'The others have had quite a nasty shock. Miss Manning and Anne . . .'

'What's the matter?' Patti stopped abruptly. She looked at the others, taking in their sickened expressions. 'What's happened?'

'Iris, dear—' Maude opened her purse and thrust a note into Iris's hand. 'The Off-Licence, if you please—'

Iris started for the door immediately, feeling that she did not wish to listen to the explanation that was about to ensue. Already, her too-vivid artist's imagination had been supplying details: the murky black of the tunnel, the blurred grey streak, the spurting crimson, the pale horrified faces, the—

'I beg your pardon.' Major Entwistle stood aside to let her pass. Although he stood almost at attention, there seemed to be an inward tremor beneath the soldierly surface. His face was white and a small tic lifted the left side of his mouth in an uneven sporadic rhythm.

'Did you come through Oxford Circus?' Iris asked, knowing the answer before he gave it.

'Why, yes, I—I tried to.' His mouth twitched upwards in a parody of a one-sided smile. 'But they weren't sending the trains through. There was a long hold-up and then we had to get out and find an alternative route. It appears there had been some sort of accident—' His mouth twitched again. 'The guards weren't very forthcoming. I dare say we'll have to wait and read about it in the morning papers—'

'You needn't wait that long.' Iris gestured towards Maude's door, still invitingly ajar. 'Some of them were closer to it than you were—'

The image of Anne's white, shocked face rose in her mind. Anne, who had not said a word.

'Go in and have a drink—' She gave Major Entwistle a gentle shove in that direction. 'They'll tell you about it.'

'But you—' He hesitated, mouth quivering. 'You're *not* going out tonight?'

'Just for fresh supplies,' Iris assured him. 'I'll be right back.'

She realized suddenly that she did not want to be out alone in the dark tonight.

CHAPTER X

Hither, page, and stand by me,
If thou know'st, then telling . . .

The boy and the man had been taken to hospital, accompanied by a policewoman who would remain with the boy until he fell asleep. After that, it would be up to the night nurses if the sedative didn't hold and the child woke screaming in the night. Even that might be preferable to the nightmares he might have if he slept.

'Christ! I'm glad that's over!' Preston said.

Knowles nodded. It wasn't over, it was just beginning, but he knew what his sergeant meant.

'It's our villain again,' he said, with certainty.

'You can't be sure of that.'

'I'm as sure of it as I can be sure of anything. Or would you rather think we have *two* maniacs roaming around our manor?'

Preston shuddered. 'It could have been an accident,' he said hopelessly.

'You heard the little boy. He says he looked back over his shoulder at the crucial moment and saw a gloved hand hit his mother in the small of her back—' He spread his hand and aped the unconscious pushing gesture the boy had made each time he told them his story.

'But he couldn't say who'd done it. He couldn't even say whether it was a male or female hand.'

'Did you expect him to be able to? With his mother plunging away from him into the path of the oncoming train? Even if he'd noticed, odds are that the shock would have driven it from his mind. He might remember something more that might help us . . . later.'

'How much later?'

'After a good night's sleep. After a few sessions with the psychiatrist . . .' Knowles shrugged his shoulders and admitted it. 'Maybe never.'

'Probably never,' Preston amended. He looked at the paper cups of congealing coffee on the desk and wondered when, if ever, they'd feel like eating and drinking again. 'I'll admit one thing,' he said. 'It's got our villain's authentic touch—it's nauseating.'

'It's also spur-of-the-moment *and* using the materials at hand. It's got his delicate hoof-marks all over it.'

'If it isn't an accident—and the boy could have been wrong. Or mistaken—there's a lot of pushing and shoving going on as a train comes in. It's a wonder there aren't more accidents. But, if it isn't an accident—what do we do?'

'We *say* it was an accident.' Knowles sighed heavily. 'We've got to keep the lid on this one. The public is beginning to get jumpy now that the media have started hinting about it. But all the other killings have happened in isolation, so they still think they're safe as long as they don't find themselves alone with any stranger. Can you picture what would happen if they knew that our maniac had changed his method of operation and they weren't even safe in a crowd any longer?'

"Strewth!' Preston perched on the edge of the desk, which was nearer than the chair, as his knees threatened to give way under him. 'Shouting "Fire!" in a packed cinema wouldn't be in it!'

'Precisely.' Knowles nodded. 'Panic—sheer panic. That's the next thing we'll have to contend with if this gets out prematurely. The media would go raving mad—and the public wouldn't be far behind.'

'I don't know as I'd blame them.'

'Nor would I, but there's no denying it would be all we needed to jam up the works thoroughly. We'd have the telephone ringing constantly with reports of suspicious sightings, the crank calls would zoom upwards, we'd get a few more confessions from those customers who are always ready to take the credit for someone else's crime—'

'Why do you suppose they do it?' Preston interrupted.

'Who knows? Maybe an overload of guilt about something—or someone—else, maybe they think they could use a nice free holiday at Her Majesty's expense, maybe they have dreams of selling their story to *News of the World* and making a fortune.' Knowles shrugged. 'Don't ask me. The one you should have asked was that psychiatrist, but he's gone now.'

'He'll have his hands full.' Abruptly, they both remembered the way the woman's husband had collapsed. After the initial incredulity at hearing the news, he had accompanied the constable to the police station with the docility of shock to help the police with their inquiries and to reclaim his son. Still enveloped in the protective isolation of shock, he had embraced a child as dry-eyed and unbelieving as himself, and confirmed that his wife had had no enemies. Not real enemies.

They had not really expected that she had. Suburban feuds did not usually end in blood and brains spewn across the underground rails at Oxford Circus.

He had even taken calmly the news that his wife had been pushed off the platform. If his son had said that was what had happened, then that was what had happened. His son was not a liar.

Somewhere about that point, the door had opened and an accredited psychiatrist from the Home Office had joined them. In their various ways, they had been delighted to see him. The emotional tension in the atmosphere had been threatening to build to a point beyond the handling of the unqualified. While they continued to question the bereaved as gently as possible, the policewoman had gone over to talk quietly to the psychiatrist. They had both been shaking their heads.

There remained the still necessary formality of identifying the body, but that had to be left until considerably more tidying up had been done on it. Meanwhile, a constable had brought in some of the parcels they had retrieved from along the tracks—the least blood-stained of her Christmas shopping.

Curiously, it had been the most innocent-seeming item, the broken fishing rod, that had cracked both father and son wide apart.

'It was supposed to be a surprise,' the little boy wailed. 'You shouldn't let him see it before Christmas!'

'Oh God! Oh God!' the father choked. 'We got one

for you last week. She was going to surprise us both—
so that we could go fishing together. In the spring!'

They had clung together and the tears had come in
great racking sobs. Knowles had lifted the phone to
order the ambulance and the policewoman and the
psychiatrist had stepped forward, both looking more
cheerful. Once the storm was over, the long work of
rehabilitation could begin . . .

'That psychiatrist has his work cut out for him,'
Preston observed.

'And so have we,' Knowles said. He reached for
the telephone. 'We'd better start checking through
the statements that have been transcribed so far.
Highly unlikely that we'll find anything useful, but
you never know.'

'You don't think our villain hung around to have
his statement taken?'

'Not for a minute. There were several trains on adjoining tracks in and out before they got the area cor-
doned off and the machinery halted. The ones who
hung around were the sensation-seekers, the curious,
and—just possibly—a few responsible citizens who
thought they might have something to contribute to
an investigation. Our villain was back in his own
snug little bolthole long before our chaps got around
to taking down the names and addresses.'

'Expecting that it would be written off as an accident,' Preston brooded as Knowles spoke into the
phone.

'And it *will* be—' Knowles replaced the receiver.
'Unless we come up with something positive from the
witnesses. If not, we'll eventually nail him for one of
the others and this will be an unwritten item on the

charge sheet. He'll know—and we'll know—but it won't be necessary for a conviction.'

'*If* we get him,' Preston said gloomily.

'You go along with the theory that the mad are smarter than we are, do you? Or do you favour the theory that he'll be possessed of such strength that he'll tear apart any of us—dogs and men—who hunt him down, and escape into the night?'

'I think it may be even worse than that,' Preston admitted reluctantly. 'I think there's a good chance he's so crazy he doesn't even know he's crazy. Perhaps whatever went wrong inside one corner of his mind will right itself again. Perhaps he doesn't know he's doing these things and, if his balance is restored, he'll never know he did them.'

'Ah,' Knowles nodded judiciously. 'You favour one of the more obscure theories in the Jack the Ripper annals. It's a possibility. You'll pardon me if I prefer not to think about it. In that case, we might never catch him. And I'd rather not be the mug with an un-solved series of murders like that on my record.'

'You admit it *is* a possibility?'

'Of course I admit it. It's always a possibility. But there's another possibility—and a more likely one, I'm afraid. Suppose our villain just goes on getting worse—until his brain snaps completely? Perhaps in Oxford Circus Underground Station again—perhaps Victoria—perhaps in one of the department stores crowded with Christmas shoppers.

'In that case, my friend, we'd get him. Red-handed. We'd catch him in the act. But, before we did, he might have perpetrated one of the worst bloodbaths in the history of crime.'

CHAPTER XI

On the fifth day of Christmas...

My head is so much better this morning that it is almost impossible to remember the agony I have gone through during the past few days. I scarcely dare to believe the improvement, and so I move slowly, cautiously, fearful of jarring it and starting off that dreadful screaming pain again.

The sun is shining, as well. Palely, it's true, and with dark clouds threatening in the distance. But, for the moment, all seems well.

Ought I to use this respite, I wonder, to try to do the last of my Christmas shopping? Or would it be safer to avoid the crowds, to do something pleasant and peaceful? A walk in the park, perhaps? Or a theatre? Some of them have matinees this afternoon. That might be pleasant. It has been such a long time since I've been to the theatre. Not since Mother died—but I mustn't think about that. It will upset me again.

I must try to stay relaxed. I really do feel so much better today. It would be a pity to do anything to spoil this lovely calm feeling. Although, curiously, it seems to be growing and strengthening.

Dare I hope? Could it be permanent? Could whatever has been wrong lately somehow have righted itself? How marvellous, if it were true. No long hours waiting in a doctor's surgery, no pills, no drugs, no fear of operations. The very thought of such freedom is making me feel stronger, happier, more buoyant.

Yes, it could be true. It is not beyond the bounds of possibility. Today, nothing can upset me. I am free. I am happy. I am—

What are they staring at over there in the window across the way?

How I loathe them! Always spying! What do they think they can discover? My life is an open book.

Those foreign fools! How brazen they are—and how stupid! Do they imagine I can't see them standing behind that thin curtain? Do they think I can't feel their eyes boring into me?

No! No, I will not let myself be upset. They're not worth it. This is too nice a day to spoil. I shall simply draw the curtains—There, and I hope they realize that's meant for them! And now I shall forget them. They're beneath contempt. Someday, someone ought to—

No! I must stop thinking about them. They must not be allowed to spoil this lovely day, this day which has been given to me like an early Christmas present, so bright and shining out of the dark wrappings of the past few weeks. This is going to be a perfect day—*my* perfect day.

Perhaps I'll do both. A little shopping this morning and then a matinee this afternoon. Aren't they having a Gilbert and Sullivan season at one of the theatres? They usually do at this time of the year. So nice for the children, and the adults enjoy it, too. I can remember going with Mother a long time ago. Yes, I must get a paper and look it up in the theatre section. I'm sure I saw it advertised somewhere.

And, tomorrow, if the weather remains reasonable, perhaps I can have my walk in the park.

How dark it is with the curtains drawn. How hard to remember that outside the sun is shining. Already this shining day seems to begin to recede. I must not let it.

It's all their fault—those people across the way! Those frightful, prying people. Why can't they mind their own business? Why do they have to nose about and spoil other people's lovely day with their nastiness?

No! I have determined that they shall not upset me. Perhaps I ought to make that my New Year's resolution: that I will not allow other people to upset me so much. I must not feel these things too deeply. Mother always said that I was over-sensitive. Yes, that must definitely be my New Year's resolution.

How lovely to be making plans again. To discover that I am looking forward to the New Year instead of dreading it. Yes, I am definitely improving. It makes all the difference when I am free of that terrible grinding ache deep in my skull.

I can hear Iris talking in the hallway—voices carry so in this house. Dear Iris. Such a nice girl, with a smile and a pleasant remark for everyone. Although, rather often, it is more a question than a remark. One must admit that often perhaps *too* often—our dear Iris is rather more curious than one would prefer.

Of course, she's not to be blamed for that. Poor girl, it must be quite dull for her, cooped up here for most of the day. Naturally, she takes an interest in everything going on around her, in the lives of the other people in the house. It is just that one some-

times feels that such a close interest is . . . perhaps
. . . unhealthy.

For her, of course, not for us. She ought to get out
more and be with people her own age. There are too
many older people in this house. I feel it myself.
There are moments when one older person is one too
many.

Is the sun still shining outside? Perhaps I might
risk a quick peek, not opening the curtains—just pulling them aside slightly . . .

They're still there. That ghastly woman and one—
perhaps two—of her revolting children. Staring across
at me. Staring, staring, staring . . .

How dare they! Do they imagine the rest of the
world is a free peepshow for them? I ought to report
them to the police! One has a right to a certain
amount of privacy.

But the sun is still shining—I must cling to that.
That is the reality. Nothing else must obscure that. I
must continue with my plans for the day. This lovely
day.

But first I must go out. I must pass through the
front hall and pause and speak to dear little Iris.

Dear little *nosey* Iris . . .

CHAPTER XII

O'er the fields we go, laughing all the way . . .

The tenants were all in a good mood this morning.
Thankful for small mercies, Iris switched off the vacuum cleaner and prepared to pass the time of day
with Patti, who was coming down the stairs with an
anticipatory smile on her face.

'Friday, glorious Friday!' Patti took the last three
steps in a single leap, landing with a thud beside Iris.
'*And* classes are over until the New Year. Isn't it
lovely?'

'Lovely,' Iris agreed, feeling quite cheerful herself.
She had two invitations to office parties at fashion
firms which were starting to use her work regularly
and a luncheon date with a client who was likely to
trail the enticing aspects of a permanent job under
her nose again. She would probably elect to remain a
freelance, but it was nice to be asked. Yes, next week
looked like being a happy and expansive one all
round.

'Isn't your sister arriving soon?' she asked Patti.

'Tomorrow,' Patti agreed. 'I'm going to do the long
haul out to Heathrow to welcome her and bring her
back. She won't believe it when she sees me there—she
knows how I hate to get up in the morning. I
wouldn't do it for everybody.'

'Well, she *is* your sister,' Iris said.

'The only one I've got—' Patti's face shadowed, the determined gaiety dimmed. 'In fact, we're all each other has, since my mother died.'

'And Pammi will be here in the morning—' Hastily, Iris offered distraction and saw Patti's face regain some of its brightness.

'That's right. We're going to have a super holiday together. There's so much I want to show her. We probably won't have time for everything. I'll let her choose what she wants to see—it's her holiday, after all. But we most definitely will want to get to a couple of theatres and—'

> *As someday it may happen,*
> *That a victim must be found …*

The piercing, but cheerful, whistle echoed down the stairs.

> *I've got a little list,*
> *I've got a little list …*

Major Entwistle came into view and stopped whistling abruptly as he saw them at the foot of the stairs.

'Ah, good morning, ladies.' He seemed no less cheerful. 'And how are you this beautiful morning?'

'It *is* beautiful, isn't it?' Iris said quickly. It was rare to see the Major in such an expansive mood, although everyone had been so uniformly cheerful this morning that it did not surprise her. Perhaps the Christmas spirit was catching up with them all, or perhaps it was merely the weather. Whatever it was, it was to be encouraged.

'And all the better for seeing you two, my dears.' The gallantry was a trifle strained, but there could be no doubt but that he meant it. He beamed at them both impartially. 'Looking forward to our party, are you?'

'It's going to be fun, I think.' Patti beamed back at him. 'Pammi's dying to meet all my fellow lodgers—she's heard so much about you from my letters. She says it's going to be the high spot of her trip.'

'Well, well, we must make sure that it is.' Major Entwistle raised a hand to his moustache and seemed only just to restrain himself from twirling it. 'Can't have a little gel coming here all the way from Canada and find it an anti-climax, can we?'

'She never would,' Patti assured him. 'Just being here would be enough by itself. And when she sees Trafalgar Square and Big Ben and all of that, she'll die. She'll simply die! I only hope there's some snow. Then it's just like living in the middle of a Christmas card.'

'Rather an uncomfortable mode of life, I would have thought.' The Major smiled. 'Well, mustn't stand here all morning gossiping, pleasant though it is. Must do some Christmas shopping. A bit late, but better late than never—' He moved off. 'Nice to waste a bit of time with some pretty girls again, though.'

He began whistling again as the front door closed behind him and Iris laughed softly. Although still faithful to Gilbert and Sullivan, the Major had changed his tune and the door closed on a sprightly rendition of:

> *Oh, what a situation for*
> *A highly susceptible Chancellor . . .*

'He's marvellous, isn't he?' Patti sighed. 'Just like something out of Dickens. I can hardly wait for Pammi to see him. She'll simply die!'

'A bit later than Dickens, I think.' Iris thought ruefully that it was amazing how old Patti sometimes made her feel. And what a good thing the door had closed behind the Major before she made her comment. Alas for the poor Major's attempt at gallantry. It was as well he did not know what he reminded Patti of. Dickens, indeed!

'Oh, you know what I mean,' Patti said. 'But he's right. I shouldn't hang around here talking, either. This is going to be my last chance to get some little things for Pammi—stocking-fillers, you know, I've got her main presents. But I won't be able to pick up anything else with her in tow.'

'Off you go, then,' Iris urged, aware that Maude's door was opening and feeling that the conversation would become too prolonged if someone else joined in. She was rather anxious to finish her household tasks and get on with some shopping of her own this morning. From now on, the stores would really be packed with the last-minute rush, and panic buying would clear the shelves of everything reasonable—and some fairly unreasonable items that would doubtless be turning up at the exchange counters after the holiday.

'See you later—' Patti hurried off, still with a spring in her step. Iris thought that Pammi would be pleased with the improvement in her sister. Although Patti still seemed to have her high days and low days, one could chart a noticeable buoyancy over the past few months. It was to be hoped that the Christmas season would not throw her back into the doldrums again. But, presumably, that was what Pammi had feared and was why she was joining her sister for the holiday.

'Time's running out—' Maude appeared in the doorway. 'And the shops will be running out of everything. This is the last weekend before the holiday. Do you think we have enough on hand?'

'We have enough for an army,' Iris assured her automatically. Maude had a tendency to flap about unimportant matters, but could usually rise to any emergency. With the store cupboard she kept on hand, she could have provided a festive dinner for all the invited guests several times over.

'I don't know . . .' Maude frowned. 'I think I'll just go out and take another swoop around the shops. I'd hate to run out . . .'

'You won't—' But the front door had already closed behind Maude. It was unlike her to dash off without a longer preliminary chat, but the urgency of the season induced a madness in everyone. At least it was a pleasant madness. Maude had looked quite happily harassed.

Humming softly to herself, Iris restored the vacuum cleaner to its closet under the stairs and prepared to go off and do her own last-minute shopping.

CHAPTER XIII

On the sixth day of Christmas ...

I have always loved Queen Mary's Rose Garden. Even at this time of year and after the sleet and snow of the other day, there are still brave blossoms clinging to the stems and proudly showing colour against the dull grey of earth and sky.

But the earth should not be grey. It should be a deep dark brown, almost red. It should be rich and fertile to mature the fragile growing things, to nourish them and encourage them to grow and bloom, to send forth their colour and their scent to enrich our impoverished world.

Oh, I see. How frightful! It's those litter louts. One finds their traces everywhere. Even here, there's no escape.

It's not a true grey. It's the overlay of pulp and detritus—paper handkerchiefs, plastic coffee cartons, old newspapers, bird droppings, bits of fluff and feathers, unidentifiable objects fallen to the ground and lost in the vast extensive compost pile of the earth. Eventually they'll become earth themselves, silt, another layer for archaeologists of the future to dig down through, recognizing the twentieth century by its peculiar debris before burrowing below it to the cleaner, neater eras of the Bronze Age and prehistory.

Oh, yes, they'll always recognize the twentieth century by the extent and the depth of our filth.

Just look at it! And the Park gardeners must have already been round this week, trying to tidy up.

And it's not just the paper and plastic—they'll eventually disappear . . . in a few centuries or so.

Oh no. It's all the metal bits. Look at them! Profaning the landscape. Everywhere. The bottle caps, the tins, the metal pull rings—everywhere. *They* won't melt, flow, resolve themselves. Oh no—not them. They're there to stay.

Even in Queen Mary's Rose Garden. In Regent's Park. There's nothing sacred, nowhere immune.

Those metal pull rings—how ghastly! And yet, strangely familiar—reminiscent. What *is* it they remind me of?

Long ago. Yes, that's it. My first job. When I was still in my teens. I haven't remembered that for years.

And yet, as the sun comes out and strikes against the metal pull rings, it all comes back to me. So alike—and yet, not alike at all. But there's something about them that takes me back—

The Post Room. Yes, that was it. Every afternoon, when the juniors carried the post down to be stamped and sealed—there *he* was. There *it* was—gleaming wickedly on his finger.

It was a ring—and yet, *not* a ring. A heavy metal loop slipped over his finger and, jutting out from it, a sharp curved blade. For cutting string, for slashing open parcels, for—

Yes, *that's* the resemblance, the memory. Those metal pull rings—different, and *not* so different, after all. They're sharper than they look, I'll be bound.

Yes, of course, they are. Look at this one I've just

picked up, looking so harmless with its blunted triangular projection. Yet, if it were used in the right way, if it were just a *little* bit sharper—

I've always carried an efficient nail file. Mother used to laugh at me for being so pernickety. As though it were not quite proper to be equipped for Life's minor emergencies, like a broken fingernail, or a need to saw through a bit of string, or—*any* crisis which might suddenly require a saw, a smoother, a sharpener—

Yes. Yes, it works quite well on the soft metal of the pull ring tab. It's brighter and sharper-edged already. Yes, I'm sure one could slice through cord or heavy paper with it now. How interesting. And the ring *does* fit over one's finger, just like that other ring in the Post Room in those early days. Things don't change as much as we think they do. They only seem to change.

Like the rose garden, the realities endure. At least, one always hopes so.

Oh no! No! Not today. Not *here!* This is a place of peace—or should be. Are they allowed to bring those filthy transistor radios in here?

Not that they'd care whether they're allowed to or not. Just look at them. Louts! Yobbos! Racing through the garden, shouting, cuffing each other, drowning out their own transistor with their noise. They've come down for some football match, I suppose. They're just the type.

And—yes—they're drunk, too. At this hour! I suppose they've been drinking all the way down on the train from whatever Northern city they've come from. Who's playing today? I can't remember. Perhaps it's not a game, at all. Perhaps they're down for the day on a firm's outing. Or to do some Christmas shopping at the London stores. It doesn't matter. What matters is that they're here.

Disturbing the peace. Profaning the atmosphere.

Why is there never a Park Attendant around when you want one?

The one with the transistor is the worst. Look at him! Stumbling, falling-down drunk. Disgusting! It would serve him right if he never got up again.

Yes. Yes, even the others seem to think that. He's fallen again and they're just letting him lie there.

No, no, they're picking him up. No, they're not. They're just moving him off the path and on to the grass beside one of the rose-beds.

What was that one of them said? His accent is so thick I can't understand the words. But the others are laughing. It seems to be some joke about putting him to bed in the rose-bed.

Yes, they're covering him with his coat and they've put the transistor by his head. He's laughing, too, but he isn't able to get up.

They'll come back and collect him later. I understood that. And now they're going off and leaving him. I believe they really mean it.

That *has* to be the ultimate in litter louts—leaving one of themselves strewn all over the ground!

Not able to get up—but still able to make a nuisance of himself. He's turning the transistor even higher—and it's tuned to some frightful pop station, with a thumping, shrieking discordancy hammering out from it.

Hammering—*like my head. No! No!* It's started again. And it's all *his* fault!

Perhaps, if I asked him to turn the transistor off.

Or, at least, turn it down. No! No, it wouldn't work. He'd only tell me *I* ought to go away, leave the rose garden to him and *his* kind. He might even grow insulting, abusive. No, I can't ask. Perhaps I *ought* to leave. Others are. There goes that respectable lady walking her dog, and the nice young students are leaving, too. No one wants to mix with *his* sort. I believe they're afraid of him.

Even just lying there, unable to get up, he's terrorizing everyone in the vicinity. It oughtn't to be allowed! Why doesn't the Park Attendant come along? There'll be no one left in the rose garden soon. Except him—and me.

I ought to leave, too. But my head . . . *my head.* It's not only aching, but dizzy, too. I'm afraid I'll fall over if I get up. How humiliating that would be. People might think I was no better than *him.*

But it's time for me to leave, in any case. There's some place I have to go, somewhere I have to be . . . If only my head would stop aching for a moment, I'd remember. I'm sure I would.

I must stand up now. Very carefully. Making no sudden move which might worsen my aching head— or draw attention to myself.

I must walk slowly, casually. The only way out of the rose garden will take me past him. His eyes are closed now. Perhaps he has passed out. With any luck, I'll be past him before he wakes again.

No, no, he's stirring. His eyes are opening. And I'm nearly beside him. If he turns his head, he'll see me.

No, he's looking in the other direction. Now he's searching for something in his pockets. Another can of beer.

What a sharp nasty sound it makes as he snaps it

open—like a shot. And the beer has spilled all over the nearest roses. Beer isn't good for roses, although I suppose it can't do them much active harm. There's something that *is* good—very good—for roses, but I can't bring it to mind at this moment.

And now he's turning the transistor higher still! Is it any wonder that I can't think properly? Who could concentrate with that insistent, throbbing, hypnotic beat interrupting their thought processes? How it cuts into my path. He did it deliberately! And look at him—lying there with that slack-mouthed grin—defying me to complain about it!

Well, I shan't allow him to get away with that! I'll pick up that tab, and march over with it, and drop it right on top of him. No matter if he does seem to have gone to sleep again!

I wish my head didn't throb so much. It's getting worse, the closer I get to that terrible blaring transistor.

There! He's not going to open his eyes, even though he know's I'm standing right over him. It's another form of defiance!

I'll drop the tab right on his face—*that* will make him react. Or perhaps I'll slide it down inside his collar, where his scarf has fallen away and his fat pink neck is exposed to the wind. It will serve him right if he catches pneumonia.

Oh! The noise! And look, I'm so distracted that I haven't picked up *his* pull tab at all. I still have the other one looped around my finger—the sharpened one.

My head! The noise! But I mustn't turn off the transistor. The sudden silence would attract attention.

Besides, I think I'm beginning to remember something—the hypnotic beat of the music is bringing it back to me. Yes, I do. I remember where I'm supposed to be going. And I must hurry. I'll be late.

Oh yes, and I remember something else, too.

Blood makes an excellent fertilizer for roses.

CHAPTER XIV

To certain poor shepherds in fields where they lay . . .

'It were a joke, like,' the boy insisted desperately. 'It were supposed to be a joke.' He had been repeating the same statement, with minor variation, for hours, each time with the same desperate intentness. It appeared not to be a question of wanting to be believed, so much as some primeval theory that, if he said it often enough and earnestly enough, it would be true. His friend would rise to his feet, the gaping wound in his throat would close and disappear, and they would all laugh heartily at what had, after all, turned out to be a consummate jape.

'It were—' The sob swelled in his throat and he swallowed it again, trying to put across his point. 'It were only a joke.'

'We coom back—' Another of the lads reinforced his ringleader's statement with the argument he, too, had been reiterating since they arrived at the police station, 'we coom back as soon as t'pub closed. Just like we meant to. So as he wouldn't catch cold, nor nothing. We *coom* back—' He raised tearful, unbelieving eyes to the watching, listening policemen.

'We *coom* back—and he were *gone*.'

Not gone—*missing*, but gone—*dead*. That was the word none of them could bring themselves to use.

There were three more of them huddled together in a corner of the room. They were the less vocal ones, no less shocked and horrified, but unable to put words—any words at all—to their feelings. That was why the other two had been the acknowledged leaders.

Detective-Superintendent Knowles wondered where the dead boy had stood in the pecking order.

'It were only a bit o' fun, like.' Perhaps he'd been a bully, a football hooligan, a menace, when the day started. Perhaps they all had. But now they'd slammed up against the grim realities of life and death, of practical joking and irony, of their own mortality.

The muggers mugged. They would never be the same again. Life was no longer their oyster, it was an underbrush of lurking menace. They weren't the young lions roaring through the quaking jungle any more, they were now quaking themselves—prospective victims, like the rest of the world. Only random chance stood between themselves and the abyss.

One of their number had already gone over the edge.

'We *coom* back,' the second-in-command insisted, unable to understand why others had not been able to play the game. 'Joost like we meant to—We *coom* back—' It *should* have made all the difference—but it hadn't. None of them would ever be so young, carefree and trusting again.

'All right, lads.' Despite himself, Knowles was in sympathy with them. They weren't yet out of their teens. They would spend the rest of their lives trying to understand what had happened to them—and why. And they never would.

Perhaps there was no answer. Perhaps, as organized religion assured them sanctimoniously, they would understand everything—once they had passed beyond the veil themselves. It was of precious little comfort to them in the here and now.

'Can we go over it again, please?' Detective-Sergeant Preston was also sympathetic but, as the policeman closer to their age, had been cast as the heavy. He tried to frown, but without much conviction—the two younger ones looked as though they might burst into tears at a harsh word, and he couldn't face that. He gave them a weak smile instead.

'Take it from the time you walked into the rose garden. Did you notice anyone in particular? Anyone acting suspiciously? Anyone even looking a bit odd?'

They all shook their heads. They had been over this ground before. They had noticed nothing.

They had been a self-contained unit. Other people were supposed to notice *them*—it wasn't for them to admit that anyone else existed anywhere around them. *They* were the centre of attention. It had never occurred to them that it might be better—safer—to move through the world without attracting too much attention. That fear, envy, hatred, violence might accompany attention.

They were wiser now, and older, unable to remember their youthful selves of just a few hours ago. The former world had shifted, tilted, and sent them hurtling through space and time, with nothing to cling to, no landmarks to recognize. They were lost—perhaps irretrievably.

'Why don't we have a cup of coffee?' Knowles suggested. 'And perhaps a pastry?'

They recoiled—each and every one of them. It was

their first instinctive reaction. As though he had offered cyanide and arsenic pasties.

'Ta—' The ringleader pulled himself together and remembered the manners he had left behind him in the North. 'I—I wouldn't mind a cup of coffee—' He swallowed drily. 'But I—I couldn't eat nothing.'

Given the lead, the others murmured agreement. Knowles met Preston's eyes and nodded. Preston nodded back and slipped quietly out of the room. As he shut the door behind him, he was aware of the general atmosphere of relaxation. They hadn't noticed that the shorthand-writer was still there in the corner of the room.

'Nothing you can remember at all, lads?' Knowles urged hopefully. 'No little thing, at all?'

They shook their heads. 'There were a good few people about, at first,' one of them admitted. 'But they started to leave while we was larking about. There weren't nothing extra about any of them, though. They was just ordinary, like.'

Just an ordinary madman. Unnoticeable—until he barricaded himself in his flat with a shotgun and let fly at the world.

If their quarry would only do that, they'd have him. But he was too clever. Or not quite mad enough.

'Why'd anyone want to do a thing like that to our Tom?' the ringleader burst out, shaking his head in the disbelief that would never leave him. '*Who'd* do it? He never did nobody no harm in his life. It joost isn't possible—' He broke off, facing the impossible again. It *had* happened. It was done and could not be undone.

'We'll get the devil, lads.' There was no comfort that could be offered them, yet Knowles did his best. 'I promise you, we'll get him.'

He hoped that he was not a liar.

CHAPTER XV

We three kings of Orient are . . .

'I wish to do the correct thing.' Puzzled, but game, Ahmed confronted Iris. 'However, I am not sure what the correct thing may be. I do not wish to offend against your customs.'

'Oh, you needn't worry,' Iris assured him. 'Everyone realizes you're not English. People will make allowances—'

It had been the wrong thing to say. He gave her an offended look and drew himself up proudly.

'I do not wish allowances made. I wish to do the correct thing. It is even more important *because* I am not English. I do not wish to appear the ignorant foreigner. I will not have them laugh at me.'

'Oh no.' Iris tried to retrieve the situation. 'No one would dream of laughing. This is a time of peace and love and kindness. You've heard the expression, "Peace on earth, good will to men—"?' She paused anxiously wondering whether, in view of the usual delicately-balanced situation in the Middle East, this might be taken as an obscure form of criticism.

But Ahmed nodded gravely. 'I have heard this expression,' he confirmed. 'What I wish to know is the proper way of expounding it.'

'Er, yes,' Iris said vaguely, wondering exactly what

he meant by the statement. Like most foreign students, Ahmed's grasp of the English language was archaic rather than idiomatic. It was not always easy to decipher what he meant from what he had actually said.

'You understand that I must study throughout most of the holiday period,' he said earnestly. 'Much as I wish to participate with the rest in Mrs Daneson's plans, this is necessary to me. I must make good grades in my examinations.'

'Quite right,' Iris said, grateful for a statement she could understand. 'I think most of us are going to be working or studying over the holiday. I have a commission from a magazine to finish myself. Maude's invitation is just for Christmas Day itself, you know.' She wondered if he visualized a week-long revelry on Victorian lines.

'The afternoon and evening of Christmas Day, really. Drinks beforehand, and then Christmas dinner, perhaps a few games or songs, afterwards. You could leave early, if you liked, but I don't imagine it will last much beyond eleven in the evening, or so.'

'Ah.' His face lightened. 'That would be satisfactory. Just the afternoon and evening. Of Christmas Day itself.'

'That's right,' Iris said. (What *had* he been imagining?) 'For the rest of the holiday weekend, we can do as we like. I mean ' she clarified 'you can do as you like all the way through. You don't *have* to come, just because Maude has invited you. I'm sure she'll understand if you'd rather not—'

'No, no,' he said quickly. 'That will be excellent. I *wish* to attend, to learn of other customs. When my studies are finished, you understand, I am destined for the Diplomatic. It is to the good of my country that I learn of foreign ways and customs. And then, after my studies here are completed, I go into the Diplomatic Corps.'

'How nice,' Iris said blithely. 'Then you'll have diplomatic immunity.'

He went pale and took a step backward. Then his face grew thunderous and he advanced on her.

'Why do you say a thing like that?' he shouted. 'How dare you make these insinuations? Why should you believe I ever need diplomatic immunity?'

Because I've seen the way you drive. Iris vividly recalled the day she saw Ahmed at the wheel of his cousin's Ferrari, careering down Baker Street with a fine disregard of traffic lights and crossing pedestrians. But she didn't voice the thought. She had obviously been undiplomatic enough.

'I'm sorry,' she apologized quickly. Ahmed was still advancing. She would be backed against the wall in another moment. 'I didn't mean to upset you—'

'Then why do you say these insulting things?' He was not appeased. 'You have no right to speak this way!'

'I'm sorry,' Iris said again. 'Really, there was no offence intended—' With relief, she heard the front door open and footsteps coming down the hallway.

Ahmed heard it, too. He stiffened warily and seemed to fight an impulse to turn and see who was coming. 'Ah, well.' He forced his features into a smile, but his eyes still smouldered. 'This is not the conversation we intended. We appear to have lost our way.'

'That's right.' Iris managed a shaky laugh. At least he had stopped advancing.

'It is right,' Ahmed declared, a bit louder than was necessary. The footsteps were coming closer. 'We ought perhaps to return to the beginning. Where were we?'

'I believe we were discussing "Peace on earth, good will to men",' Iris said firmly. She craned her neck, looking over Ahmed's shoulder and hailed reinforcements with delight. 'Good evening, Mr Stein. How are you?'

'Good evening, my love. You're discussing my favourite subject, I hear. Peace on earth, good will to men—and even to you, Ahmed. Shalom.'

'Good evening,' Ahmed said stiffly, obviously calling upon all his diplomatic expectations to force the words from his lips. 'I trust you have had a good day, Mr. Stein?'

'Don't be so formal,' Mr Stein said, a wicked glint in his eyes. 'Call me Isadore.' (His friends called him Jake.)

'No, thank you,' Ahmed said. 'It would not be seemly. You are much older than I.'

'You'll catch up,' Mr Stein said. 'Of course—' he shrugged expressively—'I may not be around when you do, so why not jump the gun now? Live a little.'

'No, thank you,' Ahmed said again. 'I must return to my studies now.' He gave Iris an awkward bow and managed to slide past Mr Stein without actually focusing on him. His steps grew swifter as he ascended the stairs until, by the second flight, he was practically running.

'Routed again!' Mr Stein said gleefully, rubbing his hands.

'That's very wicked of you, Mr Stein.' Iris tried to

keep a straight face. 'I ought to make you apologize to poor Ahmed.'

'Apologize—for what?' Jacob Isadore Stein opened his eyes so wide the eyeballs were in danger of popping out. 'What did I say? I invited him to call me by one of my given names and not be so formal. There's a law against *that* now?'

'It wasn't that.' Iris knew she was fighting a losing battle. She usually was, with Mr Stein. Furthermore, she was going to giggle at any moment. 'It was the way you did it.'

'Do? What did I do? Did I spit in his eye? Did I throw up? Did I even frown? You know your trouble, my pretty maid?' He leaned forward and took her chin between his thumb and forefinger, pinching just a trifle too enthusiastically.

'You're suffering from too much Christmas spirit,' he diagnosed. 'An overdose—and there's still a week to go. I might almost—' he stretched his features into a parody of a smile that came dangerously close to being a grimace—'call it *overkill*. You must relax, take plenty of rest, and nourishment—or I won't be responsible for the consequences!'

Suddenly he, too, advanced uncomfortably close. The game was on the knife edge of turning into something more serious.

Once again, the front door opened and slammed unashamedly shut. Two sets of footsteps approached rapidly and stopped.

'Oh!' Anne Christopher said. 'I didn't realize anyone was about.' She sounded as though she would not have come in if she had realized it.

'Only us, darling.' Mr Stein swung around avidly, as though he had caught the odd note in her voice.

'You don't call us *anyone*, do you? Come in, come in.' He motioned her forward, staring shamelessly beyond her. 'Don't be shy.'

'There's nothing to be shy about.' Anne raised her head proudly and moved forward. 'Iris, this is my friend, Tom. He's spending the holiday with me. Tom Imutu.'

'How do you do!' Mr Stein rushed to shake hands, as enchanted as any village gossip at this turn of events. 'I'm Jacob Stein.'

'How do you do?' Tom Imutu seemed a trifle bewildered at having been introduced to an Iris and finding himself shaking hands with a Jacob.

'And Iris Loring,' Anne said pointedly, disengaging him from Mr Stein's grasp and directing his attention to Iris.

'How do you do?' Iris tried to elbow Mr Stein aside. 'I'm glad you could join us for the holiday.'

'Thank you,' Tom Imutu said.

'You're Chinese!' Mr Stein was beside himself with delight. 'Are you studying English over here?'

'Probably I ought to be,' Tom Imutu said. 'But I'm not. I'm studying the restoration of antiques.' He raised a hand, forestalling the question that was evidently inevitable. 'Furniture, paintings, fabrics, books. Conservation and restoration. This is the best country to learn it in. Your things have had so much more time to deteriorate in than ours.'

'But China is a much older civilization—' Mr Stein was puzzled. 'Unless, of course—' his face cleared— 'you want to know the very latest methods—'

'I'm not Chinese,' Tom Imutu said patiently. He was obviously familiar with this attitude, as well. 'I'm American. Japanese-American, actually.' He smiled and gave a parody of an Oriental bow. 'That explains the slant eyes, doesn't it?'

'Tom—' Anne said warningly. She seemed nervous. Iris wondered if Tom Imutu concealed a formidable temper beneath that bland and smiling exterior, or whether Anne was just generally nervous at introducing her rather exotic boy-friend to her fellow lodgers.

'Japanese-American!' Jacob Stein was enchanted. 'What a United Nations party our Christmas Day is going to be!' He paused anxiously. 'You *are* coming to the celebrations? You two don't want to be alone all the time?'

'We'd love to come. It was very nice of Mrs Daneson to invite me—a stranger. Are you sure it's all right?'

'I've told you it is!' There was impatience in Anne's voice.

'Of course it is,' Iris said. 'Maude will be delighted.'

'The more the merrier,' Mr Stein chimed in. 'Just like we were all discussing when you came along. Peace on earth, good will to men.'

'See that there is,' Iris murmured.

'You're worried?' Mr Stein faced her with exaggerated innocence. 'Ahmed and I are not going to fight the Arab-Israeli conflict all over Maude's dining-room. At least, *I'm* not. With Arabs, you can never be sure.'

'In that case—' Tom Imutu grinned—'it sounds as though you might be glad of some neutral observers to help keep the peace.'

'Just what I said—the more the merrier.'

Also, *there's safety in numbers*. The random thought took Iris by surprise. Even if Ahmed and

Jacob Stein were actually to come to blows, surely there wouldn't be any *danger* in the situation.

'Okay, then,' Tom Imutu said. 'I'd love to come. We really appreciate the invitation.'

'Tom—' Anne was tugging at his sleeve, urging him towards the stairs. He seemed disposed to settle down for a long conversation.

'Yeah, okay, honey.' He shrugged off her hand. 'But I want to *contribute* something to the party—you must let me. I won't feel right about it, otherwise.'

'That's so.' Mr Stein swung to face Iris again. 'Just what I was about to say myself. What can we bring?'

'Well, I don't know.' Iris hesitated. 'I think Maude has everything pretty well organized—'

'Ah yes, she would.' Mr Stein sighed. 'Our dear Maude is always so totally in control of her situation, herself, her world. One can only envy her.'

'I don't know what to suggest,' Iris said. 'Ahmed wanted to know the same thing.'

'Maybe we all ought to have a consultation,' Tom Imutu suggested. 'We might be able to come up with a bright idea for a surprise.'

'What a splendid notion,' Mr Stein applauded. 'And I have an idea already. But we will need Ahmed's cooperation. A consultation is just what's required.'

'Perhaps Tom could leave his case upstairs, first?' Anne was a trifle acid.

'My dear child.' Mr Stein patted her arm. 'I *do* apologize. I get carried away. By all means—' he turned to Tom Imutu—'go and get settled in. And *then* we'll have our consultation.'

CHAPTER XVI

On the seventh day of Christmas . . .

Suddenly, the house seems filled with strangers. I don't like it. Why are they all here? What are they doing, planning? Why are they always huddled together, plotting, scheming? What are they up to?

They say it's to do with the Christmas party. Do they really expect me to believe that?

Oh, I pretend to. They try to involve me, and I smile and nod and agree. Then, when I walk away, I can hear them laughing. They think they've thrown me off the scent. They must think me very stupid.

Even the long-term residents are part of it. They've changed. They aren't so nice as they used to be. I don't think I like them any more.

I wish they'd all go away. I wish everyone would go away and leave me alone.

Peace. That's all I want. Peace and quiet. Why is it so hard to find?

Perhaps I ought to lie down and try to rest for a while. Although I feel perfectly well, every now and again I suspect I may not be quite recovered yet.

And pressure doesn't help. All that rushing around I did yesterday. *Having* to be somewhere at a certain time. It makes my head ache. It *did* make my head ache. I still feel dizzy when I try to think about, to remember—

No, it's better not to try to think, not to try to force myself to remember. What should there be to remember? It was just an ordinary day. I did my errands. I felt rather harassed about getting everything done in time, but I managed it. Nothing important happened—nothing worth remembering. Let it go—don't even try.

But why should I be so tired? I slept late this morning. It's Sunday. The pressure is off. Nowhere I have to be, no special time I have to be there. Peace.

And this is Christmas week. Christmas is on Friday, and that means a nice long holiday. Friday to next Tuesday, with the whole country closed down. No shops open, no newspapers printed, no post collected or delivered, no businesses open.

I like it. No one can get *at* you. The whole city sinks into a sort of state of suspended animation that must be as close to the timeless peace of the original event as is possible for the modern world to achieve.

But there's Monday to Thursday to get through before that haven is reached. That's the part I don't like. '*The runup to Christmas*', they call it. And that's just what it is. Run, run, run. Crowds, people pushing and shoving, getting progressively more bad-tempered as the supplies in the shops go down and the prices go up and they can't find what they want. Last-minute shoppers, rushing about buying things they hate for people they don't care about. It's all a nightmare.

The mere thought of it makes my nerves tighten and my head begin to throb. But too many aspirins are bad for one. I mustn't take any more. Perhaps I shall simply have an early night. Sleep late, even, in the morning. Yes, sleep. That's the best idea. For some reason, I feel quite exhausted.

But I can't relax . . . I can feel eyes . . . watching me. You can't mistake that feeling. Something unseen . . . crawling all over you.

Where is it coming from? I'm alone in this room—and yet, I *know* I'm not imagining it.

Just be quiet. Stand still. Don't turn your head. Don't let them know you suspect. Move your eyes only. Slowly. And check the possibilities.

The door—it's closed and locked. The key is still in the keyhole. No one could possibly be looking through the keyhole.

The closet. No. I hung my coat in it when I came in last night and it was empty then. And the door has been locked. No one could be hiding in there. I would have heard them, sensed them, been aware of them, long before this.

The window, then. *Turn slowly. Appear unconcerned.*

Yes—that's it! The house across the way . . . again. Look at them—pretending to be hanging decorations in their windows. Decorations—in the windows at the back of the house! And putting them up so late. I've walked down their street. I know they put the decorations in their front windows days ago.

Decorations—that's a great excuse this time of year. They're spying on me, that's what they're doing. Again. As usual. They're *always* spying.

This isn't the neighbourhood it used to be. It's gone down recently. Very recently. Ever since *they* moved into that house. Cheap, vulgar and shoddy—I don't care how much they had to pay for that house. It takes more than money to acquire taste.

Just look at what they've done to it. The disgusting drum of paraffin standing in the corner of the garden—ruining the looks of it. Even with the window closed, I can still smell that paraffin. It pollutes the atmosphere. They shouldn't be allowed to keep it there.

Probably they're not. It must be just the sort of thing there are laws against. It can't be safe having that much paraffin so close to dwellinghouses. Someone ought to report them to the police. That's the trouble with the world today, no one wants to take the responsibility for helping to keep order and make sure that the laws are enforced. Too afraid of being thought officious, or perhaps of making enemies.

I couldn't do it, of course. I'm sorry, but I simply could not bring myself to report them. Someone ought to, though. Before there's a dreadful accident. The whole community could be endangered if anything should . . . happen. If that paraffin drum caught fire . . . exploded.

It doesn't bear thinking about! People have no right to put other people into danger.

And little Iris would be in most danger. She has the basement flat—the garden flat. That flimsy fence separating the two gardens would be no protection.

Oh! Of all the insolence! They've seen me watching them as they hook their paper chains across the window—and they're *waving* at me. Trying to act innocent, trying to pretend they aren't spying—just putting up decorations.

I ought to—

No! No, I mustn't let them suspect I recognize

their real intentions. I must smile back, I must wave pleasantly. I must act the way they expect me to act.

This is the Season of Brotherly Love, after all; of peace on earth, good will to men. Smile and wave again before I move away from the window, out of their view.

I hate them all.

CHAPTER XVII

It came upon a midnight clear . . .

' "Sunday, Bloody Sunday"—whoever said that was dead right, I reckon.' Detective-Superintendent Knowles raised his arms above his head, swung his legs out from behind the desk, and stiffened in a mighty stretch.

'Never mind, it's Monday in a few more minutes.' Preston offered dubious comfort, taking the opportunity to move away from the desk himself. They had both been hunched over it for hours, going through their own reports and the reports from other precincts on the bizarre series of murders taking place all over London.

'Monday—and another inquest to attend. Courtesy of our own pet looney.' Knowles contracted into brief limpness, then stretched again. 'Held at bloody dawn to try to keep the Press from noticing what's going on. Is it worth going to bed at all? That's what I want to know.'

'Which one is this?' Preston asked.

'Can't you keep track, either?' Knowles blinked at the piles of reports spread untidily across the desk. 'The newsagent from Soho. That's tomorrow's inquest. Then, on Tuesday, we want to drop in on the inquest for the solicitor from Middle Temple. That will be at the crack of dawn, too. The local police are all co-operating with us. They don't disagree with our theory that it's all the work of our own little chum.' Knowles snorted. 'Why should they? If they can pass it over to us, so much the better for them. Believe me, if I had anyone I thought I could pass it on to, I'd move so fast I'd leave you breathless.'

'Perhaps he isn't ours—' Preston tried to be cheerful. One of them ought to be. 'Perhaps he's one of those characters who doesn't want to foul his own nest. He may really be living next door—in St John's Wood, or the Edgware Road, or Queensway—' The idea was momentarily enticing. 'There've been a lot of nasty things happening in Queensway's patch over the past few years. Not all of them solved yet, either.'

'Regent's Park Lake . . .' Knowles intoned slowly. 'Baker Street . . . Queen Mary's Rose Garden . . .' His voice was like the tolling of a bell. 'All of those in our patch. And the others . . . on the borders: Soho . . . Oxford Circus . . .' He sighed again.

'No, the villain's ours. I know it. I feel it. Sod your computers, *I'm* getting the printout from the marrow of my bones.' He crossed to the window and frowned out into the blackness.

'He's out there somewhere in the old Borough of St Marylebone. I *know* it. He's lying low right now, biding his time. But he'll strike again—and again—until we stop him. He's out of control and we've got to find him and grab him. But . . . where the hell *is* he?'

'Two inquests in a row—' Preston had a gloomy foreboding about who would be expected to take notes and remember all the salient details. 'That's a bit stiff.'

'And don't forget our poor little girl from the chemist's shop in Baker Street,' Knowles said. 'In common humanity and with respect to the feelings of her family, we'd like to get that one out of the way before Christmas, if we can. That means Wednesday or Thursday.' He paused in gloomy contemplation. 'If we can get the paper work done in time to fit it in.'

'But the others will have to wait until after Christmas,' Preston said. 'The woman at Oxford Circus tube station—they *might* go for an accident verdict. There's only the child's word for it that someone in the crowd pushed his mother. Perhaps that *was* an accident.'

'Don't you believe it.' Knowles snapped. '*I* don't. It was our little chum, changing trains on his way home—to St Marylebone. He's striking closer to home nearly every time now. *And* at more frequent intervals.'

'Well,' Preston continued to try to look on the bright side. 'At least, nothing has happened today.'

'How do you know?' Knowles would not be cheered. 'Maybe we just haven't heard about it yet. There may be something waiting to be discovered to-morrow morning—*this* morning—when the cleaners go through some building. Or later, when the office staff arrive.'

'But it's Sunday,' Preston protested.

'And you think on the seventh day *our* villain is going to rest? I don't. I don't think he's got any rest in him. I think he's getting worse and will go on getting worse until—' Knowles broke off.

'That's where I stop thinking. For all we know, he's worse already. How do we know how many other victims we may have scattered around the city—written off as accidents, or undiscovered? It works both ways, that fact about the victims being in places and jobs readily accessible to the general public. Perhaps that's only the reason *those* bodies have been found. Perhaps there are others, lying in empty houses, or on abandoned building sites. It can be days—or weeks—before the neighbours begin to notice that they haven't seen old so-and-so around for a long time and think of mentioning it to us. You know that.'

'It could be.' Preston nodded gloomily. It was amazing—and infuriating—the length of time people could go along soothing themselves that everything was probably all right. That Aunt Nellie or Cousin Jane might have had a sudden invitation to go and visit some other relative and, in the excitement of the moment, had forgotten to cancel the milk and papers.

As Knowles had said, it didn't bear thinking about.

'It may not be that bad.' Preston fought a rear-guard action. 'Look, maybe Saturday's victim was the last—in our neck of the woods. The holiday has started already for some people. Who's to say that wasn't our bloke's last shot in the locker before he goes home for Christmas? Regent's Park is close to the main stations: Euston, King's Cross, or even Paddington. Who's to say he wasn't on his way to catch a train to Edinburgh . . . or Cornwall . . . or somewhere far away—'

'And safely out of *our* manor?' Knowles gave a bitter laugh. 'Any more fairy stories like that and I'll begin to have my doubts about you, lad.'

'It's possible.' Preston went on the defensive. 'You

were the one who kept saying that our villain retreated to the bosom of his unsuspecting family after
each murder—'

'When I said that, I meant that he had a family living nearby. You're talking about a family too far
away for commuting purposes. Anyway, it doesn't sig-
nify now.' Knowles wriggled his shoulders uneasily, as
though trying to dislodge an unseen burden. 'I don't
believe it any more. I've changed my mind. There's
been too much water under the bridge since I started
out with that theory—'

'Too many more murders, you mean,' Preston said.

'Yes,' Knowles acknowledged. 'Too many deaths—
and at too emotive a time of year. Christmas. " 'God
bless us,' said Tiny Tim." I don't believe our killer
has any family. Perhaps he did have once—but not
any more. Or he couldn't be behaving the way he is.'

'Maybe Christmas doesn't mean anything to him,'
Preston suggested. 'He may not even be English.'

'I hope to God he's not!' Knowles allowed honest
chauvinism to break through. 'It would be the one
bright spot in this case if he turned out not to be. Although,' he admitted gloomily, 'God knows what the
National Front would make of it if he *were* a foreigner.'

Preston shuddered. That, too, did not bear thinking about. In fact, there was not much about this case
that one could face thinking about. Yet they were not
only expected to think about it—they were expected
to solve it.

'*No*,' Knowles went on. 'I'm betting that our
maniac is a loner. Or, if he does have someone, it's
not the one he wants. If he's going back to a place he
calls home, then whoever's living there with him is ei-

ther someone he's indifferent to, or possibly even hates.

'And that gives me nightmares, too. Because maybe that hair-trigger temper has already been set off within the confines of his home.

'Maybe—' Knowles gestured widely—'somewhere out there, we have a charnel house waiting to be discovered.'

CHAPTER XVIII

O'er the fields we go, laughing all the way ...

The house echoed with the lilt of laughter. Maude looked upwards, smiling.

Sudden loud thumps and a series of shrieks faded the smile somewhat. Not quite frowning, she backed away from the foot of the stairs and waited as the noise thundered closer.

The staircase began vibrating wildly just before the two of them swung into view at the top of the final flight of stairs. Laughing, hand-in-hand, they raced down, then paused at the foot for another round of a battle which had obviously been going on for some time.

'You *don't* want to go off by yourself!' Anne protested.

'Only for an hour, I promise.' Tom Imutu struggled to free his hand. 'I'll meet you for lunch—anywhere you like.'

Maude stepped back into the shadows lest the sudden pain in her heart find reflection in her face. They were so young and so . . . joyous. They brought back memories she thought Time had buried—or, at least, dulled. She had been a widow for so many years now that she thought she had forgotten those early shining days.

But they were here before her again. Glowing in Anne's face, shining in Tom's.

Imutu. Did it matter? Everything had changed so much these days. Miscegenation was the bugbear of a previous generation, today's children were untroubled by the word. If, indeed, they had ever heard it. And as for the dreaded shame of an even earlier generation—who spoke in whispers of *mésalliance* today? To judge from the gossip columns, it had been the done thing for some time. No one gave it a second thought. ('Haven't you heard? Lady Sarah's moved in with the fishmonger.' 'Oh, jolly good. Perhaps we'll get some decent whitebait next time she invites us round.')

'I'll meet you at one—name the place.'

'That's longer than you said—you said an hour.' The laughing squabble continued.

A door closed somewhere below. Iris must be on her way to start the morning's housekeeping duties.

Maude backed swiftly to her door, turned the handle noiselessly and slipped inside, closing the door just as Iris reached the top of the basement steps.

Leaning against the door, she heard Iris's footsteps pass along the hallway. In the distance, voices broke suddenly into loud and innocuous conversation, interrupted by laughter as Iris joined them.

Maude moved slowly away from the door, still amazed at the wrenching agony. She had been free of it for so long that she had thought it would never return. Not with the raw twisting misery of a fresh wound—or scar tissue ripped away from a newly healed one. It had caught her unsuspecting, unprepared.

For so many years now, the ache had been in her head rather than in her heart.

Iris waved goodbye as Anne and Tom went out, having decided to stay together as far as Baker Street Station before they parted to go their separate ways. She winced as the door slammed violently behind them, reverberating through the hallway.

The reverberations were quickly drowned out by more laughter from somewhere at the top of the house. Quickly, before anyone came down to distract her, Iris plugged in the vacuum cleaner and got to work on the hall carpet. She did not expect to do more than make a start on it, and the babble of voices and laughter were upon her before she had done more than a few feet of carpet.

'Such energy at this hour.' Patti halted at the foot of the stairs and linked arms with Pammi.

'It's not *that* early.' Iris was determined not to be seduced into a long conversation. She was due for a Christmas lunch with one of her advertising agency clients and wanted to be on time. Not that Maude would complain if the housework were skimped, but she did not want to take advantage. She was periodically conscious of just how lucky she had been when she had looked Maude up with such happy results. Apart from which, this was going to be a week of guesting at agency and magazine Christmas parties and she did not want to begin skimping work too early.

'It is for *us*.' Patti and Pammi had been standing there, arms linked, looking, in the way that siblings did, not particularly alike. Now, on the same beat, they tossed their heads back, rocking with hilarity, and might have been identical twins. Although she had noticed the phenomenon before in members of her own family, Iris found it faintly uncanny.

'That's all right for you,' Iris defended. 'But *my* holiday hasn't properly started yet. I'm still on duty for the rest of the week.'

'Poor Maude. You make her sound like a dreadful slave-driver. And she isn't—' Patti turned to Pammi earnestly. 'Maude is *sweet*—although you wouldn't always notice it. But just look at the way she's giving this Christmas party for all of us. She really *is* a softie at heart.'

Iris glanced nervously towards Maude's door, but it appeared safely closed and soundproof.

'Iris doesn't think we ought to talk about Maude right outside her door.' Patti had not missed Iris's swift glance. 'It *would* be more convenient if Maude didn't have the ground-floor flat, wouldn't it? Then she wouldn't be able to keep track of all our comings and goings either—' Patti paused wickedly. 'It would be more convenient for *all* of us.'

'Well, *I* don't think you ought to talk about the lady right outside her door, either.' Pammi abruptly became the severe elder sister. 'You *know* you'd be more embarrassed than either of us if the door opened and she was standing there.'

'I suppose so.' Patti shrugged, admitting her sister's point, but there was still a mischievous sparkle in her eyes.

'You *know* you would.' Pammi looked at her sister fondly. 'You'd be so horrified you wouldn't know how to apologize, so you'd just get mad and it would be Ottawa all over again—' She broke off abruptly, obviously aghast at what she had let slip out.

'No, it wouldn't,' Patti said quietly, but she had gone pale. 'Nothing like that will ever happen again.'

It was apparent that neither of them could meet the other's eyes now. Whatever closet door had been inadvertently opened, it seemed that there was a skeleton of considerable magnitude lurking within.

'Of course not,' Pammi said quickly. 'I didn't mean that. You know I didn't mean *that*.'

They both glanced guiltily at Iris, who quickly transferred her own gaze to the vacuum cleaner. When she stole a glance at them, they appeared relieved to find that they had been careless only in front of someone who could not recognize a skeleton when it began to dance before her eyes.

'Eeek!' Patti suddenly slapped her hand against her forehead. 'Now look what you've made me do, Pammi—' She turned to Iris, spreading her hands in appeal. 'She's rushed me so, I've forgotten my chequebook!'

'That's the best way to go shopping,' Pammi said. 'Otherwise, it's fatal—I mean,' she said quickly, 'you'll spend too much. Especially at Christmas time. There's something hypnotic about the stores then, and you find yourself buying all sorts of things you don't want, need—or even like.'

But she was talking only to Iris. Patti had turned and hurtled back up the stairs, taking the steps two at a time.

'I'm so grateful to you all,' Pammi said. 'You've been so good to Patti—and so good *for* her. I can't tell you how grateful I am. She's nearly herself again—the way she used to be.'

'We haven't done anything,' Iris disclaimed hastily. 'Patti has been treated just like any other lodger.'

'And that's *just* what she needed. Only, I guess we couldn't bring ourselves to be casual with her. She cracked up so badly after our parents died that the rest of us were afraid—' She broke off, shaking her head. 'We were terrified when she insisted on coming over here all by herself. We were so afraid—'

'Patti is just fine,' Iris said firmly, trying to cut off the unwanted confidences. It made her feel vaguely disloyal to Patti to be listening to them. 'She was always fine—so far as I could see—from the moment she arrived here.'

'She was right, then,' Pammi said. 'About herself, I mean. She said that what she needed more than anything else was just to get away from it all, to a place where nobody knew her or what she'd been like, and to start all over again. Among strangers. And then she could find out who she really was and what she could really do. She diagnosed herself and prescribed her own cure better than all those expensive doctors, after all.'

'Patti is all right,' Iris insisted. (Was Pammi protesting too much?) 'She had a difficult time, I gather, but she's regained her equilibrium and I'm sure no one need worry about her any longer.'

'Her equilibrium,' Pammi breathed. 'That's *just* what it is. All that worrying, all those family conferences—and she's found her own way out of the woods all by herself. And it was probably better for her doing it that way, too.'

'I'm sure she—' Iris broke off abruptly. There had been a sound from the top of the stairs. She and Pammi, faces turned upwards expectantly, suspended conversation and waited.

Smiling and talking together, Eva Manning and

Major Entwistle descended the stairs side by side. Their smiles faded and their voices trailed off into awkward silence as they became aware of the girls at the foot of the staircase avidly watching their descent.

'Good morning, Miss Manning, Major Entwistle.' Inwardly, Iris cursed herself—and Pammi, too, who had really been responsible for it. She had been hoping a romantic spark might kindle between those two elderly lodgers since she had arrived here. But now they blinked guiltily, avoiding each other's eyes and looking as though they would like to run in opposite directions and never speak to each other again.

'We thought you were Patti,' Iris said quickly. 'I mean, we were waiting for her to come down—' She broke off, she was only making things worse. There was no way to retrieve the situation.

'Good morning, Iris,' Miss Manning said. She nodded more distantly to Pammi and continued descending the stairs, moving a step or two ahead of her erstwhile companion. She appeared less flustered than Major Entwistle, but one hand rose to brush at her face, as though trying to brush away flies—or the combined gaze of the two girls.

'Good morning, girls.' Major Entwistle was considerably less cordial than he had been the last time he had spoken to them—but he had been alone then. Slightly flushed, but determined, he took a couple of swift steps and caught up with Miss Manning, reaching for her elbow. This time, it was his hand she brushed away. His flush deepened.

Like strangers, they marched stiffly down the hall, no longer acknowledging each other's presence.

'Oh dear,' Pammi said ruefully, as the door closed behind them. 'That *was* unfortunate.'

'I think I'd have felt better if they'd slammed the door,' Iris agreed.

'*Nothing* could make me feel any better,' Pammi said. 'I don't know when I've ever felt so much like a busybody caught spying on the neighbours. Not even when I was actually guilty of it.'

'Oh, really—' Iris tried to lighten the conversation. 'I'm sure you've never spied on anyone, Pammi.'

'Sometimes it's necessary,' Pammi said seriously. 'For the other person's own good—'

It would be impossible to pretend that she did not know what Pammi was talking about. There was a point beyond which uncomprehending innocence became downright imbecility. Iris averted her gaze, instinctively letting it stray towards the top of the stairs. She gasped involuntarily, and Pammi looked upwards also.

Patti was standing there, looking down at them. The earlier laughter was gone from her face; her eyes were hooded; her expression shadowed.

'I found my chequebook,' Patti said. Head held high, she descended the staircase regally.

Iris and Pammi met each other's eyes with mutual consternation. How long had Patti been standing there? How much had she heard?

'We can go now.' Patti lifted her head even higher and looked at her sister defiantly. 'I'm all right now.'

CHAPTER XIX

On the eighth day of Christmas . . .

They're watching me again.

All of them.

I can *feel* it—even when I can't see it.

Even the ones who pretend to be sympathetic, who pretend to be friends, who try to act as though they're on *my* side.

They're lying. All of them.

And I have to act as though I believe them. Smile when they smile. Laugh when they make a joke. They mustn't suspect that I *know*.

You can't trust anyone. I've always known that. And now, every day proves it to me, more and more.

Yet . . . it wasn't always like this. Was it? I can't seem to remember. It's so difficult these days.

Everything seems more difficult. Even in the times when my head stops aching. But the aching seems more frequent lately . . . constant, almost. It frightens me when I think about it.

I mustn't think about it.

What *can* I think about?

The New Year? Yes, the New Year.

I can't think about Christmas. I don't *want* to think about Christmas. What have I let myself in for? All those people . . . a Christmas party. Everyone watching . . . no longer having to pretend that they aren't.

And I shall have to smile and talk and laugh and look as though I'm enjoying myself—and them. Act as though I'm having a wonderful time—wish you were here.

—*No!* I didn't mean to think about that!

I hope they won't want to play games. I don't mind if they want to sing Christmas carols, but I hate playing games. I'm always stiff and awkward and can never enter into what they persist in calling "the spirit of the thing". I hate it.

I hate them.

I must find another place to live. Soon. As soon as the holiday season is over. I meant to wait until I was feeling better, until these terrible headaches were under control. But I don't think I can stand all these frightful people much longer.

After New Year. Right after. Before I consult the doctor, even. I must find another place—

But wait. Why should *I* be the one to go? You see how these headaches blur my thinking? Let *them* go.

Yes. They're the ones who are spying, lying—interfering with my freedom. *They* must be the ones to go.

I'd be perfectly comfortable here, if it weren't for them. I always have been, in the past. I will be again. Without all of them around.

I feel better now that I have that perfectly clear in my mind.

Of course, I must bide my time. I must be fair. There is no point in worrying them prematurely. There is nothing they can do about finding alternative accommodation at this time of year. We all know that everything in England closes down in the week before and the week after Christmas. Also Easter.

But Easter is not under consideration. Easter is light years away. By Easter, everything will be settled, everything will be over.

I shall be at peace again.

But first, I must get through these terrible holidays. I *can* do it. I *must*.

It's the Christmas party itself I dread most. If only it weren't for that, it wouldn't be so bad.

The Christmas party—and the Christmas dinner. All of them will be seated around the table, smiling, laughing—jeering. I can see them now.

And every time I close my eyes, above the throbbing in my head, the roaring in my ears, I can see a sharp gleaming light.

I can see them all sitting around the table, watching.

Watching the head of the table. The succulent, browned sizzling turkey. And the bright gleaming light—darting, biting, sawing into that smooth brown surface, the moist white meat beneath.

Again and again. Smooth, neat slices falling away from the bone. One after another—until they're all gone.

I mean, until the turkey is carved, until the skeleton is laid bare. Thin white bones glinting in the firelight.

The highlight of every Christmas dinner. The inescapable climax. Inevitable.

There'll have to be a carving knife, won't there?

CHAPTER XX

He's making a . . .

'You see—' Preston tried to cheer his glum colleague. 'Nothing new happened yesterday. And nothing's happened today, either. I told you. Our villain's gone to visit the family up north, or somewhere, for the holiday.'

'The day's not over yet,' Knowles said gloomily.

'For us, it could be.' Preston let hope go to his head. 'The whole case might be over. With any luck, he'll carve up his dear old auntie while he's visiting. Or push a little cousin into the canal. Or do something inventive to one of the neighbours—and that will be it. Our troubles are over. He'll belong to the local force. In a small town, they'll be able to trace him down and light on him—'

'What makes you think it's a small town?' Knowles would not be cheered. 'It might be Glasgow, or Birmingham, or Edinburgh, or Sheffield, or—' He broke off, shaking his head. 'Our villain could decimate a good percentage of the population and be back in London before anyone noticed he was gone. Feeling all the more refreshed for his little holiday and ready to go back to work with renewed zest down here.'

'You may be right.' Preston slumped into his chair. 'On the other hand—' he tried for the brighter outlook that was in danger of slipping away—'I may be right.'

'And only time will tell.' Knowles reminded him bleakly. 'Meanwhile . . .' He picked up the pile of reports and began shuffling through it once again. Reports, statements from witnesses, results of autopsies—somewhere there must be some common factor, some clue that might help.

'You must have those things pretty well memorized by now.' Preston reached for his own pile of Xeroxed papers. 'I just about have, myself.'

'And the only pattern I can find is that there *is* no pattern,' Knowles said bitterly.

'Perhaps something will emerge with the next—' Preston broke off before his colleague's vicious glare.

'And how many more do you think we can stand by and let him rack up before we get enough clues? Perhaps, if we wait long enough, our villain will die of old age.'

'Jack the Ripper did. Died—I mean. At least, that's what they think happened to him. He just stopped—as suddenly as he'd begun. Maybe that will happen with our villain.'

'It won't exactly put any feathers in our caps if it does, will it?' Knowles pointed out. 'It will be an unsolved case on our records.'

'On more records than ours,' Preston said.

'Furthermore, it's the kind of case they'll be writing up and hashing over for the next hundred years—like your Jack the Ripper. We're just lucky they haven't started already. It's partly because the murders have been so scattered around the city and the methods used so different—'

'Holiday season helps, too. The media are looking

for nice cheery human interest stories. What pop stars are flying in to Heathrow to spend Christmas with their dear old mum and dad. Carols around the Christmas tree in Trafalgar Square. Underprivileged kiddies getting presents—'

'All right, we've been lucky so far,' Knowles acknowledged. 'But we can't count on it indefinitely. Any time now, some bright journalist is going to start putting two and two together—'

The telephone rang abruptly, startling them both. They looked at each other with grim foreboding before Knowles stretched out his hand and lifted the receiver. He listened in silence to the voice at the other end of the line.

Preston watched anxiously as the other's face grew progressively grimmer.

'Is it another?' he asked, as Knowles finally replaced the receiver without having uttered more than a couple of noncommittal grunts.

'That will bloody well teach us to speak of the devil!' Knowles snarled. 'We're slated for a Press Conference tomorrow morning. Some bleeders from the Nationals have twigged it at last!'

The doorbell rang and kept ringing impatiently. 'Wait a minute, can't you?' Iris muttered, dashing up the stairs. 'I'm coming.'

'Oh, good, I'm glad you're home.' Maude stood there, wrestling with an exceptionally heavily-branched fir tree. 'I'm sorry to disturb you, but I simply couldn't manage this any farther by myself.'

'I'm not surprised.' Iris held the door wide as Maude battled the tree into the hallway.

'It was an impulse buy,' Maude confessed with a rueful grimace.

'I'm relieved to hear that,' Iris said. 'I'd hate to think you went out deliberately to buy that—that *forest.*'

'Just balance it a moment, will you, dear, while I get my key out.' Maude tilted the tree over to Iris. 'Careful, don't let it fall—we'd never get it upright again.'

'You can say that again,' Iris muttered, trying to keep her face from being scratched by pine needles. 'Couldn't you have found something smaller?'

'I didn't intend to have a real tree at all.' Maude unlocked her flat and swung open the door. 'But I was passing that shop in Marylebone High Street, you know—'

'I know—' But Maude had gone inside. Iris gritted her teeth and began dragging the tree along.

'And so—' Inside the flat, she found Maude still continuing with her saga. 'When I saw those neighbours buying a tree. You know—those newish people, the foreigners, in the house behind us—'

'I know.' Iris gingerly leaned the tree against the wall beside the fireplace.

'Well, it suddenly swept over me. I thought, Why don't *we* make it a real old-fashioned Christmas? Tree and all. In for a penny, in for a pound!'

'I suppose we can only be thankful you weren't passing through Trafalgar Square at the time,' Iris said. 'A forty-foot Norwegian spruce would have been *too* much.'

'Although, I must say—' Maude ignored the comment—'*I* think it ought to be set up immediately. I was talking to them and—do you know?—they're going to leave it in the hallway, just inside their front door, and not set it up and do the decorations until Christmas Eve.'

'The tenants *would* love climbing over that monstrosity to get in,' Iris said. 'I'd have cheered them on if they'd deducted the cost of ruined tights from next week's rent.'

'The question doesn't arise,' Maude said regally. 'I would never have dreamed of leaving the tree in *our* hallway. Nor do I intend to leave it leaning against the wall in here until Christmas Eve. We'll set it up now. Iris, dear, I believe you'll find a tree stand in the box room at the end of the downstairs passage. At the back, behind the empty trunk that strange Egyptian left behind when he went away.' . . .

She might have known, Iris thought wryly, that she'd be left to do all the dirty work. Quite literally dirty. She looked down at her sticky, resin-stained hands and decided that a quick wipe with the turpentine cloth before washing them would be the best bet.'

And she would do *that* before she went grubbing in the decades-deep dust at the back of the box room for the tree stand. Dust adhering to sticky resin didn't bear thinking about. Why did Maude have to have these sudden brainstorms? Was she getting more eccentric, or was it just the Christmas season bringing out the sentimental worst in everyone? . . .

The tree stand, as she might have expected, had been in the farthest corner, behind a booby trap of outworn, but not discarded, household utensils.

She took her time and scrubbed the tree stand, as well as herself, after she found it. Her tights, she noted glumly, had given up the ghost somewhere between an abandoned wicker laundry hamper and the famed Egyptian trunk, which had turned out to be a mass of blistering, peeling dried leather, surprisingly heavy to move, obdurately blocking her way. With the cost of excess baggage on airlines, it was not surprising its owner had chosen to abandon it. . . .

As Iris passed through the front hallway, carrying the tree stand, the front door opened.

'Oh, Iris, there you are.' Eve Manning came in, swaying slightly, weighed down by two carrier bags which appeared to be loaded with heavy items. 'Good. I can get rid of some of this here and not have to carry it upstairs and down again.'

She deposited the bags with a sigh of relief and began rummaging in one of them. 'It's right here. I know it is. At least, I think it is. Although, possibly, it's in the other bag. I changed hands a couple of times. Although both bags seemed equally heavy—' She continued rummaging.

Iris put down her own burden and waited patiently. She, too, was glad to put it down. It weighed a ton. Of course, it would have to be heavy—iron, or steel, or something—to counter-balance the weight and height of the Christmas trees it was designed to hold.

'Here we are—' Eva Manning straightened triumphantly with a bulging paper sack. 'A little contribution to the communal Christmas party.'

'You shouldn't have—' Iris took the sack automatically. It tilted and opened, nearly spilling some of its contents.

'Just a teensy offering.' Miss Manning backed away, blushing. 'I thought—'

'Chestnuts! How lovely!' Iris looked down at the lustrous gleaming shells.

'I know Mrs Daneson has a lovely fireplace. And I thought—roast chestnuts. *So* appropriate. Just the thing for a real old-fashioned Christmas.'

It was a positive epidemic. The 'Old-fashioned Christmas' syndrome in full swing. How many others would succumb? And what would constitute an old-fashioned Christmas for *them*? At least, this idea was fairly innocuous. Iris smiled. She certainly preferred it to Maude's.

'It's perfect,' she said warmly. 'And so much—'

'Two pounds. I hope it's enough,' Miss Manning said anxiously. 'There'll be about a dozen of us, won't there? I wouldn't want anyone to go short. Do you think I ought to get more?'

'No, no, this will be enough,' Iris said. 'It will do for the stuffing, too, I'm sure. How very kind of you to think of it.'

'Oh, well, I was just passing the fruiterer's in the High Street, and these looked so good—'

'It was an impulse buy,' Iris finished for her.

'That's right.' She beamed on Iris. 'How clever of you! Of course, I was going to get something, anyway, but I couldn't think what. Until I saw these. It was an inspiration.'

'It certainly was,' Iris agreed. 'Maude will be delighted. She's been having inspirations of her own this afternoon. Why don't you—' she gestured towards Maude's door—'come and—'

'Oh no. No, I couldn't intrude.' Eva Manning backed towards the stairs skittishly. 'I just wanted to make my own small contribution. To enter into the *spirit* of the thing, as it were . . .'

'It's just right—' Iris was reassuring a departing back. With a faint sigh, she stooped to pick up the tree stand. As might have been expected, the top layer of chestnuts burst out of the bag and went bouncing across the carpet.

With another sigh, Iris put down the tree stand and chestnuts and went gathering up the escapees.

She heard the front door open, but—on the track of the last chestnut, wedged against the lowest stair rail—did not bother to look round.

'What's this?' a familiar voice questioned. 'Hunt the thimble? Starting the Christmas games already? And all by yourself?'

'Oh, Mr Stein.' She caught his outstretched hand and let him pull her to her feet.

Nothing so practical as a carrier bag for him. He was festooned with small parcels distorting every pocket and juggling an assortment of paper bags.

'Let me help—' Iris reached out as a couple of the bags seemed in danger of slipping from his grasp.

'Naughty, naughty.' He backed away. 'Little girls shouldn't go getting curious about shopping at Christmas time.'

'Oh, you haven't!' Iris exclaimed in dismay.

'Nothing, really,' he disclaimed. 'Just tiny bits and pieces. Stocking fillers, small tokens—'

'An old-fashioned Christmas,' Iris murmured.

'Exactly,' he beamed upon her. 'But what would I know about such a thing? Only from watching the television commercials.'

Iris wondered what *he* had been passing when the impulse overtook him. It was too much to hope that any of the tenants might have been passing through Hatton Garden.

'I thought I heard you talking out here.' Maude stood in her doorway. 'Have you found it?'

'Good evening, Mrs Daneson.' Mr Stein nodded to Maude and scuttled up the stairs guiltily.

'I found it.' Iris snapped on the hall light. Darkness had abruptly descended and there was nothing gloomier than for the residents to walk into a black hallway.

'Here we are.' She picked up the bag of chestnuts and the tree stand and followed Maude back into the flat, resigned to grappling with the tree again. All in the name of an old-fashioned Christmas.

CHAPTER XXI

On the ninth death of Christmas . . .

No! That's not right. Why should a morbid thought like that stray into my mind?

It's *day*—DAY . . . 'On the ninth *day* of Christmas . . .' How could I possibly think anything else?

It *is* the ninth day, isn't it? It's so dark. That's the trouble when one wakes in the small hours of the morning. What time *is* it?

Not light enough to see my watch without putting on the bedside lamp. I don't want to do that. The glare hurts my eyes. It might start the headache off again.

Besides, people can see into the room when the light is on. Those terrible people across the way. They never sleep. Our whole house is silent now and I know that I am safe here. But *they* don't need sleep. They're not like *us*.

The alarm clock—that has a luminous dial. What does it say? Quarter past six?

No. No, it's half past three. In the morning. The bleakest, coldest hours of the night. The darkness before the dawn. And I know—from how much long, bitter experience do I know!—that I shall not sleep again for hours. Not until the alarm clock is ready to go off.

Perhaps I should take sleeping tablets. But they frighten me. I don't want to surrender my consciousness to an amalgam of chemicals. And how do I know that they'd really work? Nothing else does.

Not the warm bath; not the hot, milky drink; not the boring soothing book; nor the counting of sheep . . . I shall lie awake, staring into the darkness until the sky lightens with the promise of another day—and then I shall sink into slumber so deep it is physically painful to be wrenched from it by the shrill demand of the alarm.

And today—yesterday—was such a pleasant day. Such a successful shopping expedition, with so many happy finds.

Is that a light in the house across the way?

No. No, they're too clever to show a light. But I know they're awake, too. Watching . . . spying.

But I mustn't think about that. There's no way of proving it. They're too clever . . . too sly.

I must try to think of the pleasant day. The felicitous shopping expedition. All the lovely fascinating things I found, and saw.

Not that I wanted to buy everything I saw. But some things, while not suitable for anyone on my list, were most interesting in themselves.

That brooch—badge—in the antique shop, for instance. Just a simple, almost austere, set of entwined initials: LFR. While I was gazing at it, mentally trying to fit the initials to someone I might know, I heard the owner of the antique shop answering an enquiry from another customer about the article.

LFR, it appeared, stood for London Fire Raisers—a secret Victorian society who operated an early form of the protection racket. If prospective victims did not pay them off, then they set fire to their premises. So successful—and bold—were they that they had designed the badge and fearlessly wore it. Only a few knew what the initials stood for. The police did not know—until far too late.

Yet, one has to admire the ingenuity. Such a simple procedure—but so effective.

If their demands for payment were not met, they simply stuffed oil-soaked rags through the letter box in the front door of their victims' residence in the dead of night. Then they struck a match—Lucifers, I suppose they would have been called then—and tossed the lighted match through the letter box to land on top of the oil-soaked rags.

So simple. So effective. No wonder they operated so successfully and over such a long period of time. They could be far away and unsuspected when the fire was discovered. No wonder they dared forge a badge and flaunt it in the face of their baffled foes, the police.

I didn't purchase the badge, of course. For one thing, the initials did not fit any of my acquaintanceship. For another . . .

That beastly headache is back!

Why must I be plagued like this?

Is it not enough that those frightful people in the house behind keep spying on me?

It's no use. I can't go back to sleep. I'm too upset. Even though I know they're not worth upsetting myself about.

Perhaps I ought to get up. There are sleep specialists who recommend that one get up and make oneself a cup of tea or hot chocolate. There are others who say that the best thing is to get dressed and go out and take a walk and then go back to bed.

I've never tried that. I've tried everything else. I wonder whether that might work?

Oh, it's cold. It's dark.

But it's so silent. And deserted . . . out there. No watching eyes. No listening ears. No one at all to notice what may be going on.

Yes, perhaps I *ought* to go out and take a nice soothing walk. I've never been out at this hour before. It's silly to feel self-conscious. Who is there to notice me?

The streets will be utterly deserted. No one else will be stirring at this hour.

Half past three in the morning. Well, perhaps quarter to four, by now.

But silence out there. '*In the still of the night* . . .' It can't get any stiller than this.

Even those people across the way are sleeping now. I can *feel* that they are. That must have been their last peep out of the window that I was conscious of—just before they finally went to bed.

They thought I was asleep. They thought it was safe to call off their watch.

Yes, I must get up and get dressed. I must try that final remedy—a nice long walk.

It will be perfectly safe. I am not a child to fear the unknown, unseen phantoms of the night.

Let them fear me!

My head! The ache . . .

Perhaps the air will clear it. I won't put the light on—it might alert them across the way. I can dress in the dark.

It will be nice and quiet out on the deserted streets.

Too early to meet a milkman doing his rounds. I'll see no one. No one will see me.

I can move silently through the house and slip out of the door without making a sound. And return. And no one will ever know that I was out and about in the darkness. Everyone else is still sleeping.

There are oil-soaked rags in the basement.

Iris has thrown them out. Her old paint rags. They're in too disgusting a state even for her to use any more. Soaked with linseed oil and turpentine, smeared with dirty blobs of oil paints where she wiped her brushes.

Iris will never notice that they're missing. Having discarded them, she'll never give them another thought. She'll assume they were carried away with the rest of the rubbish when the dustmen came to collect it.

Why should she suspect that anyone else might remove them? Might have another use for them?

But I must move silently.

CHAPTER XXII

Bring a torch, Jeanette, Isabella,
Bring a torch to the stable, do . . .

Iris awoke with her throat burning and the dry acrid smell of smoke in her nostrils.

Fog, she thought vaguely and turned over. Her eyes opened, closed, and opened again. They were stinging. And there was an eerie flickering red glow on the walls. She turned over again and lay there blinking, consciousness slowly returning.

Something was wrong.

The signal finally made its way through to her nerve centres. She threw back the bedclothes and reached for her dressing-gown.

As she did so, someone screamed.

Shuddering into her dressing-gown, Iris threw back the curtains and looked out into the back yard. Later, she could not explain to herself how she had instinctively pinpointed the source of danger so swiftly and accurately.

Appalled, she gazed at the spectacle across the garden.

Flames were blazing across windows—devouring the paper chains hung there as Christmas ornaments—blazing in a travesty of festive decoration. Behind them, the interior of the rooms glowed fiercely.

It was obvious that the fire was worse at the front of the house, facing on to the road. That was where the screams were coming from.

But couldn't someone *do* something?

Iris threw open the french windows and stepped into the garden, moving towards the fence dividing the properties. Perhaps, if she could climb over the back fence—

'Iris! Get back into the house!' A window was thrown open above her and Maude leaned out, shrieking instructions. 'Get back! Don't be foolish! You can't do anything!'

Iris moved forward doggedly. The heat was increasing and the smoke nearly overpowering. Was something inside the house disintegrating into deadly chemical fumes under the fusing power of the flames?

'Iris! Stop!' Maude's head disappeared and she slammed the window shut.

Before Iris had reached the fence, Maude was beside her, pulling her back. In the distance, the whoop of fire-engines and ambulances could be heard converging on the blaze.

'Back in the house!' Maude pulled Iris off-balance with a violent tug. 'It's dangerous here! They keep that paraffin drum of theirs right on the other side of the fence. You can't do any good. And if a spark falls on that paraffin drum—!'

'She's right, you know.' Major Entwistle joined them. In fact, the garden was filling as residents of the house, in varying stages of disarray, came out to see what was happening. Maude had taken the shortest route, marching directly through Iris's flat, but the others had come down the area stairs, leaving the door open behind them. Most of them were huddled just outside the door, staring in fascinated horror.

Hating herself, Iris allowed herself to be drawn back to the shelter of the house. Maude was right, she could do nothing.

'Oh dear. Oh dear.' Eva Manning kept wringing her hands. 'How awful! How frightful! Can't anyone *do* anything?'

Ahmed, Mr Stein and Tom Imutu started forward.

'Oh, stop them, can't you?' Maude clutched at Major Entwistle. 'Make them all go back into the house. That flimsy fence will be no protection at all if the paraffin goes up.'

'Everyone inside!' The note of command was in his voice and Pammi and Patti were the first to respond to it. Patti, shivering and on the point of weeping, Pammi, with her arm solicitously around her sister's waist, guiding her into the house.

'Upstairs,' Maude directed. 'We can watch from my windows. And I'll make coffee. I don't expect anyone will be worrying about going to sleep after this.'

'Inside! Upstairs!' Major Entwistle barked. 'Assemble in Mrs Daneson's quarters!' Not waiting to see whether he were being obeyed, he marched across the garden to the men trying to get into the other yard.

'Inside, you men!' he ordered. 'Now!'

In his heyday, the Major must have been a formidable figure. He was still pretty effective, Iris noted. The trio of would-be heroes had halted uncertainly—looking from the blazing house to Major Entwistle and back again.

Perhaps if anyone had appeared at one of the windows, it might have been different. But the action was obviously at the front of the house.

And the screams had stopped. Now there was only the crackle of flames and the muted shouts of firemen at the front of the house.

'Paraffin . . .' Iris caught the Major's word and his gesture towards the fence as Maude drew her into the house.

'Shut the windows and draw the drapes,' Maude said, 'before we go upstairs. That will be some protection, at least, if there *is* an explosion.'

'Someone ought to warn the fire brigade about that paraffin,' Iris said. 'They won't know about it. And it's dangerous to them—' She started for the stairs.

'We'll send one of the men round,' Maude said. 'I'll need you to help me with the coffee.'

With a backward glance at the ominous flickering glow still apparent despite the shrouding draperies, Iris followed Maude upstairs. It would be safer in Maude's flat, too. If there were a blast, the full force of it might come through the fence at ground level.

Or would it? But there was no time to worry about that right now. The others had reached Maude's flat ahead of them.

Eva Manning was wringing her hands like a latter-day Lady Macbeth, casting occasional glances towards the window. Patti and Pammi had their backs to the window, Patti was shivering uncontrollably.

'The men have gone round to see if they can help the fire brigade,' Pammi reported as Maude and Iris entered. 'Major Entwistle said they ought to be told about the paraffin in the garden and the others went with him. But—' she caught Patti, who was trying to turn to look out the window—'I don't think they can help, I don't think there's anything even the experts can do.'

'It's terrible,' Eva Manning mourned. 'Terrible—
and only two days before Christmas, too.'

'Let's not drag sentiment into it,' Maude said
briskly. 'It would be terrible at *any* time of the year.
We can only hope that it isn't as bad as it looks. But
conditions were so appallingly overcrowded in that
house—I often wondered whether I ought to report it
to the proper authorities. But, of course, one always
hesitates and—'

'And then it's too late.' Anne Christopher finished
the sentence for her. Anne was framed in the window, staring out, her arms crossed protectively. 'Before you can even realize it, it's too late.'

'The children were playing with matches, I suppose,' Eva Manning said. 'Or someone was smoking in
bed. Foreigners—' she condemned, implying that no
English people would be guilty of such lapses.

'It's so awful!' Patti burst into sobs. 'Just happening like that. In their own home. In the middle of the
night—so suddenly—no warning. There's no safety
anywhere! Not even here!'

'These things happen,' Maude said sharply.
'There's no point in brooding about it. That way
lies—'

She broke off in mid-sentence as Pammi flashed her
a vicious glance.

'Take it easy, Patti,' Pammi soothed. 'She's right.
Things like this will always happen. It's awful, it's
terrible, it's unfair—but, there you are. They still happen.'

'I know,' Patti sobbed. 'I know. But they
shouldn't—'

There were clumping footsteps in the hall outside.
Iris opened the door to see Major Entwistle leading

some of the firemen through the hallway and down the stairs. They were evidently going to try to do something about the paraffin drum from this side of the fence. Of course they wouldn't be able to get through the other house to deal with it. The fire was blazing too fiercely.

Had anyone been able to get out of that inferno? Iris shuddered and closed the door. They would find out soon enough. Major Entwistle would probably be able to report when he rejoined them.

'Patti, come and help me with the coffee,' Maude directed briskly. 'The others will be back soon.'

Obediently, Patti moved forward, sniffling into her handkerchief. The prospect of something to do seemed to cheer her. Pammi started to come with her, but Maude shook her head slightly and Pammi fell back again.

'I wonder,' Maude said, 'whether we ought to make enough for the fire brigade?'

'Do they drink on duty?' Iris asked.

'You're thinking of the police,' Maude said. 'There's no reason why the fire brigade shouldn't accept a cup of coffee.'

'They'll be too busy to bother right now,' Eva Manning said. 'I'm sure they will. And, when the fire is out, I believe they have to go directly back to their station in case there are any more alarm calls to other fires.'

'That's what I meant,' Iris said. 'They're on duty.'

'In any case,' Anne spoke from the window without turning around, 'they're really working over in the next street. The people over there will take care of them if they want or need anything.'

'I suppose you're right.' Maude gave in reluctantly.

'But I still feel that we ought to *offer*. Perhaps the firemen who are in the back garden might like—'

'They've got the paraffin drum—' Anne reported from the window. 'Thank heavens. They're bringing it back in through the house.'

'It was probably their paraffin stove that was responsible for the fire,' Maude said. 'Those things are always the cause of too many accidents in the winter.'

CHAPTER XXIII

On the tenth day of Christmas ...

I cannot believe the way time is rushing along. I seem to have lost yesterday completely. Of course, I think everyone else in the house felt the same. After that terrible, terrible tragedy right on our doorstep—well, our *back* doorstep.

And so little any of us could do about it. Although we tried. We wanted to help. But it was too much for us. It was too much for the fire brigade, as well.

For the rest of the day, we found ourselves speaking in lowered voices when we met on the stairs. It cannot be my imagination that most of us seemed to want to avoid meetings. The incident cast a pall over the entire neighbourhood. And now the burnt-out house stands there, a blackened reproach to everyone who views it. Gutted. Absolutely gutted.

Still, it *is* nice not to be overlooked.

I suppose it would be too much to hope that the Christmas party might be cancelled out of respect for the dead. We are not a house in mourning. It is not as if any of us were friendly with those people. We hardly knew them except by sight.

No, we will have the party as scheduled the day after tomorrow. Why, I even overheard that little idiot Iris saying, 'The show must go on.' Even though none of us are in show business or have any remote connection with it.

But there you are, there's no logic in any of them.

How the smell of burning hangs in the air! Wet, charred timbers and scorched plaster. A constant unpleasant reminder. After more than twenty-four hours, you'd think it would have faded away. You wouldn't expect it to remain hovering in the vicinity, insidiously creeping through chinks in the doors, constantly reminding one of terrible scenes one wishes only to forget.

The atmosphere is polluted.

Yes, that's it. Polluted. Contaminated. This house. The air outside. The whole—

That's Iris down there in the garden. What is she doing? She's carrying her sketchpad and heading straight for the hole in the fence where they chopped through to get at the paraffin drum and take it away.

That's trespassing! I'm sure it is. Not that she'd care! Ought I to rap on the window and call out to her?

No. Better not. Better just to watch quietly and see what she's going to do.

She's going to sketch that house. What's left of it. How frightful! How morbid!

And yet, I suppose, to an artist's eye, it has a certain attraction. The starkness of those blackened timbers where the roof fell in, the long narrow finger of a chimney pointing upwards into the sky.

It's just line and composition to her. The horror that led to its creation means nothing to her. Callous and indifferent—if not actually brutal.

Everyone is these days. You have only to look at the ghastly things shown on television every night or reported in the newspapers. And it seems to get worse and worse. So very different from the world that I remember when Mother was alive. Perhaps she is lucky, after all, that she is not here to see it. Whatever would she think of it all?

How long is Iris going to stay in that other garden? Has she been in there earlier to sketch? She found her way unerringly to the break in the fence and settled herself on that outcropping of stone as though she were familiar with it.

Has she been in there sketching during the hours I have so unaccountably lost? Did she ask permission to go in there and sketch? If so, of whom? The fire brigade? The police . . . ?

I don't like Iris. She's a troublemaker. Just by the sheer fact of her existence, she's a troublemaker. And a danger.

But she mustn't suspect I hate her. I must smile and be polite. I must appear to be fond of her—like all the others in the house.

Mad—all of them! Can't they see her for what she is?

I must not think about them. I must not allow myself to get upset. My head will start aching again. And the pleasantly detached woolliness that has surrounded me all day like a fog is infinitely more preferable.

It has not been an unpleasant day, on the whole. I have had a feeling of pleasant weariness—as though I had successfully completed some difficult, but necessary, task. The feeling of a good job well done and worth the exhaustion it brought.

No, it has not been an unpleasant day. Until now.

Look at her! Calmly sitting there, slashing away at

the white page of her sketchpad with that piece of charcoal. I suppose it *is* charcoal. It looks like something she might have picked up from the ground—there are so many charred lumps around—or broken off from one of the timbers, so black and menacing that they might still be smouldering.

Suppose someone saw her in there? Suppose someone from the Fire Brigade were to come back to check that nothing was still smouldering and see her there? Start asking questions?

It makes my head ache just to think about it!

Iris is dangerous. I've always known that. I've tried to overlook it because, in her way, she has been useful. But now she is becoming too much of a threat.

Steps must be taken to neutralize her.

CHAPTER XXIV

Above thy deep and dreamless sleep ...

Knowles and Preston were in plain clothes—and in hiding. By mutual tacit consent, they had found a pub well away from their usual haunts. Several drinks along, they were still racked by occasional shudders, but beginning to feel a bit stronger.

'I wouldn't be Commissioner for all the Scotch in Scotland,' Preston said. 'Imagine having to face that *every* time there's a flap on.'

'If you can't stand the heat, keep out of the kitchen.' Knowles was not quite so ready to relinquish claim to the Commissioner's job some day. 'But he earns every penny they pay him, I'll say that for him.'

'So do those Fleet Street chaps.' Preston had recovered enough to chuckle. 'Did you see their faces? A story like this dropped on their plates—and four days without newspapers coming up. I thought some of them would have a stroke!'

'With luck, they might yet.' Knowles permitted himself a wry grin. 'The television people were nearly as hysterical. They'd love to make a meal of it, but their holiday schedules are made up and ready to roll. All those expensive feature films—they couldn't afford to cancel them. All hell would break loose if they did.'

'All hell might break loose if they don't, and miss the biggest story since Jack the Ripper.'

'They *did* rather bear down on the poor old boy, didn't they?'

'But you rattled them nicely with the idea that it might be the work of some student who had now gone home for the Christmas holiday and, "he might be in Paris, Vienna or Abadan by this time",' Preston quoted reminiscently. 'That really threw them. They didn't want to start a story that might be dead—or dormant for the next few weeks. Or that might suddenly blow up in another country. Although a few of them looked as though they might be working out the angles on an all-expenses-paid trip to cover the story if it did. That was a proper red herring, and no mistake.'

'It might even be true,' Knowles allowed cautiously. 'Two days have gone by now without any fresh activity from our villain. On form, he was getting worse and something new should have surfaced by this time—if he's still around town.'

'Perhaps by this time, he's pushed someone off a Channel ferry,' Preston suggested. 'We'd never know it. It would go down as another accident. Or perhaps—' he brightened—'perhaps someone has pushed *him* off. Perhaps that's the way this case will end. He'll wind up murdered by one of his intended victims. And we'd never know that, either,' he realized gloomily. 'There'd be no way of telling he was our killer. Only that the killings would stop as suddenly as they'd started and we'd never know.'

'That won't happen,' Knowles said with finality.

'It could,' Preston insisted.

'It won't,' Knowles said. 'And I'll tell you why. Because we wouldn't be so lucky.'

'Iris, how *could* you?' Maude looked at the stark canvas reproachfully. 'It was bad enough when you were just sketching those ruins—but to *paint* them. How *could* you?'

'I think it's awfully good.' Pammi squinted at it thoughtfully. 'You weren't thinking of selling it, were you? For a reasonable price, I mean. It would be really wild to take it back to Toronto and show the gang.'

'Pammi, you *wouldn't* buy it!' Maude shifted her attack, still reproachful.

'Like a shot. It would make a great souvenir of my trip. Come on, Iris, how much?'

'Umm, forty pounds,' Iris said, preparing to bargain.

'Great!' Pammi cut the ground out from under her. 'Wrap it up, you've made a sale.'

'It's still wet,' Iris cautioned, as Pammi advanced gleefully upon her purchase. 'We'll have to wrap it very carefully if you want to take it with you when you go. And you'll have to let it dry for at least six months before you can varnish it. A year would be better.'

'As long as I can hang it, I don't care how long I have to wait to varnish it,' Pammi assured her. She didn't seem to notice that Patti was regarding her nearly as dubiously as Maude.

'Somehow, it makes it worse that you're selling it,' Maude mourned. 'And, as for actually hanging it on the wall—' she turned to Pammi—'where you can see it all the time. And remember all those poor people—how *could* you? I just don't understand young people today.'

'Well, it's history, in a way,' Pammi pointed out. 'And a piece of history I was eyewitness to. Besides, *not* painting it, or *not* buying it, wouldn't undo anything. The awfulness would still have happened, all those people would still be dead. Trying to ignore the fact doesn't change it.'

'I suppose not.' Maude shook her head regretfully. 'But you make me feel—' She broke off, raising a hand to her head.

'Look, are you sure you want to part with it?' Pammi turned back to Iris. 'It's really good. I wouldn't want to rob you of it. If you'd rather keep it—'

'It's all right,' Iris said. 'I'm going to paint some more views, from different angles.'

'Oh, Iris!' Maude was appalled. 'It—it isn't decent!'

'It's art,' Pammi assured her gravely. 'It doesn't have to be decent. Artists can't always help the subjects that appeal to them and set them going. And, you know, I think Iris is going to be a very famous artist some day.'

'I'm going to try,' Iris said seriously, already looking past them to the ruins of the burned-out house. 'I'm sorry, Maude. I don't mean to offend your sensibilities but—but there's something about that house, that gutted hulk, looming black against the bright blue sky. Austere, grim, even horrible, I know, but I can't help it. I want to do some more studies of it. In oils.'

'It's morbid!' Maude shuddered and turned away. 'But I suppose you know what you're doing. I'd never have believed anyone would want to buy a painting like that, but you've sold it already. Obviously you know your own business better than I do.'

'It's art,' Pammi said again. 'And art isn't always pretty. This picture isn't pretty, but it's strong.' She seemed to become aware that her sister had been standing by silently all this time. 'What do you think about it, Patti?'

'It's good,' Patti said slowly. 'I can see that. But—but I agree with Mrs Daneson. *I* wouldn't want it hanging on any wall of mine. It would remind me too much of that awful night.'

'Oh.' Pammi looked at her uncertainly. 'Well, in that case, I'll put it away whenever you come to visit. How's that?'

'That's fine,' Patti said. 'I'm sorry, Iris—' Belatedly, she remembered that the artist was standing beside them. 'I don't mean to be rude or anything, but—'

'Don't worry, I'm not insulted,' Iris said. 'But do you mind if I leave you now and get back to work? I'm longing to start another canvas, and it gets dark so early these days. I don't want to waste the light.'

Not quite waiting for their murmur of agreement, she hurried away.

'It's all right, I suppose.' Maude looked after her uneasily. 'But I wish she wouldn't be so obsessed with that dreadful house. It's silly, I know—' she gave a nervous laugh.

'But, in some strange way, I feel as though she were tempting Fate . . .'

CHAPTER XXV

On the eleventh day of Christmas . . .

Christmas Eve. At least, the day before Christmas. Tonight will be Christmas Eve.

Nearly time.

I shall be pleased when it finally grows dark and I know that this day is over and there is just tomorrow to struggle through.

Boxing Day won't be so bad. The long holiday is nearly over then. Even though the next day will be a public holiday, as well, the festivities will be dying down. Everyone will be getting bored with the feasting, and the time off, and the trying to be pleasant to tiresome relatives and friends. They'll be looking forward to getting back to work. So will I.

But, before tomorrow, there is today.

And there goes Iris again! Straight through the gap in the fence to that gutted hulk of a house. She *must* stop it! People will begin to notice. To ask questions.

There are other people over there, too. I can see their pale figures through the empty windows as they move about the house. What are they looking for? What do they hope to find?

There's nothing there. Those dreadful people are gone. I can live in peace again—without them spying on me.

Of course, there are other spies. Here in *this* house. Iris is one of them.

She needn't think she's fooling *me* with her talk about painting and carrying those canvases and tubes of paint around with her. I know what she's *really* up to.

Who are those people over there? What is she reporting to them?

Why can't everyone leave well enough alone? Those terrible people are gone, their house gutted—and there's an end to it. They won't be back. Everyone ought to be grateful instead of making such a fuss. No one really liked them, so why must they be so hypocritical about it now?

They're all as bad. Especially Iris. With all there is to do on the day before Christmas, why isn't she in the kitchen helping? That's what she's supposed to be here for. There are a thousand things that need doing before a big dinner party—everyone knows that.

I wish I hadn't thought of the dinner party. I don't know how I can face it. Sitting down at a table with all those dreadful people—and Iris. Laughing and talking with them, trying to pretend that I'm enjoying it. The very thought of it makes my head begin to throb.

Trying not to let them know what I really think of them. Trying not to show how much I despise them.

I really must take an aspirin, my head is aching so. And there seem to be shooting lights flashing behind my eyes. Sharp, cruel lights. Like the reflected light glancing off the blade of a carving knife.

There'll be a carving knife on the dinner table tomorrow. A long, sharp, gleaming blade, ready to carve the turkey. So much a part of the Christmas scene that no one really notices that it's there at all. No one thinks anything of it.

I wish I could get it out of my mind.

I can see it so clearly, and those bright blinding flashes of light radiating from it as it is wielded. It makes me feel quite ill.

But none of the others will know or care about that. Selfish—every last one of them! They'll sit laughing and eating, paying no attention to anyone else.

They need to be taught a lesson. Someone ought to shake them out of their complacency and their self-satisfaction—and their spying.

They're terrible—all of them! They ought to be punished. They deserve to be . . . To be . . .

Gutted. Like that house.

CHAPTER XXVI

O Tannenbaum, O, Tannenbaum ...

'It's our villain!' Knowles lifted his head and glared around the blackened hallway as though he expected to catch the arsonist still lurking in the smoky shadows. 'It's got his pawprints all over it. I *know* it's his work. I can feel it! I can smell it!'

Automatically, Preston drew in a deep breath. He began coughing. The harsh acrid air seemed to have seared his lungs all the way down to the pit of his stomach. What must it have been like at the height of the blaze?

'He's somewhere close by. He *has* to be.' Knowles gazed outward through the charred oblong hole that had once held glass and been framed by net curtains.

'It looks like it.' Preston got the cough under control and breathed more cautiously. 'He hasn't gone home for Christmas, after all.'

'This *is* his home. This area. This neighbourhood.'

'Some neighbour!' Preston said. 'But we're closing in on him.'

'Not yet,' Knowles disagreed. 'He's narrowed the field, though. We suspected it before, but now we know it. He's somewhere on our patch.'

'And he's getting more dangerous by the minute. Just our luck.'

'Everyone had bad luck on this one. The fire needn't have been so bad—except for that damned Christmas tree.' Knowles kicked at a charred balustrade which had fallen to the floor.

'That tree being there was hell's own luck,' Preston agreed.

'He couldn't have *known* it was there, could he?' Knowles asked the blackened blistered ceiling.

'That would mean he knew the layout of the house,' Preston ventured. 'Perhaps he'd been a visitor—or even lived here.' It was not unknown for people to set fire to their own homes—although such cases were mercifully rare in England. Of course, all the people in the house were really—despite their passports—foreigners. 'I suppose someone's checking the insurance angle?' he asked hopefully.

'All taken care of.' Knowles was still brooding about the Christmas tree. 'God knows how long it had been cut before being sent to market. And there it stood in the corner—drying, full of pitch, slowly turning into pure tinder. All it needed was one spark. They never had a chance. It fell across the doorway, you know, blocking any chance they might have had of getting out. If it hadn't been for that—'

'You believe someone knew about it, then,' Preston said.

'We'll find out,' Knowles promised darkly. 'Right now, he thinks he's safe. He wasn't to know that the fire would jump from the point of origin, leaving it relatively intact. If he *didn't* know the layout on that night, he had every right to expect that the incendiary material he pushed through the letter slot would blaze away on the hall carpet, ignite the carpet itself, and destroy the evidence along with the house.'

'At least,' Preston said, 'we're dealing with an amateur.'

'At arson, yes. At murder, no. We're dealing with the same maniac we've been dealing with all along. The means are different every time and we may never know the motives. Not even after we catch him. But, my God! he's an opportunistic bastard!'

'They think the fire started around four a.m., don't they? That doesn't sound a very opportune time to me.'

'And that's where we've got him!' Knowles glared at his sergeant challengingly. 'Or got a strong lead to him,' he amended. 'This time, it's different. This time, he's moved closer to home. It's not only that he knew too much about his victims, it's also the method he used.

'Each time—before this—he's used something close at hand to improvise a murder weapon. But this time, look at what he's used: a lighted match thrown on top of oil-soaked rags. No one carries oily rags around with him on the off-chance that he might want to use them. No, he lives somewhere close by.'

'Or works around this area,' Preston said. 'Possibly in a garage.'

Knowles nodded. 'We'll have a better idea when we get the lab report and know what kind of oil was saturating those cloth fragments. But my money says he's living around here, not working. It happened too late—or too early—to coincide with any work shifts. We haven't any all-night garages in the area, but any insomniac might decide to take the dog out for a walk at any hour.'

'Just a nice quiet private citizen minding his own business,' Preston said bitterly.

'Until he runs amok,' Knowles agreed.

'He's amok enough for any of us right now.'
Preston looked at the skeleton ash of the Christmas
tree. 'The question remains: how do we find him?
He's still privately amok, as you might say. If he doesn't
run publicly amok—in front of witnesses—he can keep
this up indefinitely. This random striking down of
innocent citizens at any hour of the day or night,
with no warning—'

'And no chance for them to escape,' Knowles said
in a dead voice.

'Perhaps the lab report—'

'The lab report will be late, as usual. They're understaffed and it's Christmas week—if you remember.
Other people are taking holidays. Even when we get
the report, it will depend on whether they had
enough of the residue for all their tests.'

'We were lucky there was anything left at all. If the
fire hadn't made that jump to the fir tree—'

'If it hadn't, more people might still be alive. The
fire might have burned itself out with no worse damage
than a hole in the carpet and a scorched front door.'

'Perhaps we ought to consider the possibility that it
wasn't our nutter,' Preston suggested cautiously. 'This
was outside the general pattern in other ways, too.
Most of his malice has been directed against one indi-
vidual and with certain results. This was against any
or all of the residents in this house and it was by no
means certain that any of them would be hurt, or
anything worse than badly frightened. It could be
someone else.'

'Three people are dead and four are still in hospital, two of them critical. The others are frightened,
all right, but as puzzled as we are. There seems to be

no rhyme or reason to it.' Knowles turned his head slowly, quartering the empty hallway again.

'Except, perhaps, in one disordered mind. One disordered—*nearby*—mind. We'll question the survivors again. Perhaps something will emerge; one memory might spark off another; someone might remember something—' Knowles broke off, frowning through the glassless blackened aperture that looked out upon the back garden.

'We ought to start questioning the neighbours, too—' Preston halted and turned to follow his chief's gaze. At the far end of the garden, a girl was slipping through the hole in the fence. She was carrying what looked to be a large flat board. 'They're not putting up a For Sale sign already?' Preston murmured. 'They might wait until the embers are cool.'

'Wrong sort of board and approaching from the wrong direction.' Knowles watched her progress. 'Unless I miss my guess, that's one of the neighbours coming to look things over now.'

'Not returning to the scene of the crime, I hope,' Preston said. She was a pretty girl but, when you had one like this on your plate, you never could tell.

'If she is, it's the first time.' Knowles turned abruptly, heading for what remained of the back stairs. 'But she must live nearby. Let's have a word with her and find out if there's anything she can tell us.'

CHAPTER XXVII

All is calm, all is bright . . .

An attack of belated guilt drove Iris from her painting and back to the house. It *was* Christmas Eve, after all, and Maude could use some help with all the work. Besides, it was clouding over—perhaps they'd have a White Christmas this year—that would be rather nice. Good painting, too—if a bit Christmas-cardish. The burnt-out house would banish the Christmas card look, though.

More likely, it would just rain. Iris dumped her painting kit on the table, leaned the wet canvas against the wall in a row with the other canvases, and went upstairs.

She had scarcely had time to report to Maude when the first tap came at the door.

'I thought I'd leave these under the tree now.' Eva Manning stood in the doorway, clutching a precariously balanced stack of matchbox-sized gaily wrapped parcels. 'Just to get them out of the way. And, of course, ask Maude if there's anything I can do to help. She must be so very busy today. You *both* must be.'

'Come in.' Iris stepped back and Eva Manning moved past her into the living-room.

'Oh, how lovely!' she exclaimed, seeing the tree. 'Maude always does everything *so* beautifully.'

'Doesn't she?' Iris agreed, remembering her struggles with the topmost branches.

'I'll just put these here—' Eva Manning distributed her presents along the wide fans of pine needles where they perched like multicoloured exotic birds. 'And here—' She had just arranged them to her own satisfaction when there was another tap at the door.

'Good afternoon.' Major Entwistle smiled down at Iris. 'It occurred to me that this must be an exceptionally busy day for you and Mrs Daneson. I thought I might drop by and offer my services. There must be any number of things that need doing—'

'You can both peel chestnuts for the stuffing!' Maude appeared in the kitchen doorway, evidently having heard more than one might have expected at that distance. But that was Maude—there was little that went on in the house that she didn't know about, although she seldom saw fit to display the extent of her knowledge. 'I've just boiled them and we can all have a glass of sherry while they're cooling enough to handle. Then—to work!'

'It's very kind of you both to volunteer.' Iris tried to soften Maude's rather brusque acceptance of their help.

'Not at all,' Major Entwistle said. 'It makes it seem more like Christmas to be *doing* something. I always helped Mother out in the kitchen on holidays.' He smiled apologetically. 'My wife, that is. I always called her Mother, although, after the first couple of miscarriages—'

'Quite!' Maude thrust a glass of sherry into his

hand, cutting off further potentially embarrassing confidences, and then gave one to Eva Manning.

'Christmas *is* coming together and helping one another, isn't it?' There would be no confidences, embarrassing or otherwise, from Eva Manning. She moved the conversation smoothly on to another plane. At least, she tried to.

'When one *can*.' Major Entwistle glanced sadly towards the gutted house at the back. 'I can't help feeling that there ought to have been something more we could have done—'

'Who were those people I saw you talking to?' Maude challenged Iris. 'They seemed to have had a lot to say.'

'They were asking questions, mostly.' Iris accepted her own glass of sherry. 'They're police officers working over there. I wasn't able to be very useful, though. I scarcely knew these poor people by sight, let alone whether they had any enemies, or not.'

'Enemies?' Eva Manning's glass trembled. 'Why should the police ask questions like that? Why should they be there at all?'

'They don't think the fire was deliberate?' Major Entwistle seemed equally disturbed. 'Surely they can't imagine any human being could be responsible for that—that holocaust?'

'That's unthinkable!' Eva Manning protested. 'No one could have done such a thing on purpose. It's—it's monstrous!'

'I know, but—' Iris shrugged. 'I suppose the police have to look at everything from a suspicious angle. It's their job. And, if there *is* a firebug starting up in this district, I'd prefer that they begin working on it sooner rather than later. After all—'

Someone else was at the door. Iris broke off and went to open it.

'*Hail, hail, the gang's all here,*' Patti chanted, bursting into the room with Pammi. 'We came to see if you needed any help, and we find you whooping it up as though tomorrow weren't Christmas and you hadn't a chore in the world.'

'Everyone else had the same idea,' Maude said. 'But don't worry, there's enough work for everyone. Come and have a drink and then I'll find something for you to do.'

'First—' Patti gave Iris a frankly appraising look—'I want to know what you were doing with those two gorgeous men in the garden . . . ?'

It was a question frequently repeated during the remainder of the afternoon as the other tenants drifted in and out with offers of help.

Iris began to feel as though no one in the house had had anything to do that morning except watch her movements. She had had no idea that her painting had become such a popular spectator sport. Everyone was aware that she had been talking with the investigating officers in the garden. And everyone was curious about the questions they had asked—and her answers.

'Honestly,' Iris protested finally, 'we were just talking. I didn't take notes.'

'Next time, you'd better,' Patti said darkly. 'I'll bet *they* are.'

'Surely there won't be a next time!' Eva Manning gave a little cry of dismay. 'They've asked their questions and found there's nothing Iris can tell them. There's nothing any of us can tell them. Surely, now, they'll go away.'

'They can't,' Major Entwistle spoke with growing melancholy. 'Too many people have died.'

Patti whimpered softly.

'There'll have to be a full investigation,' Maude agreed. 'If only to demonstrate that the police are working.'

'But they *are* working.' Iris could not let that pass. 'And working hard. Those two were telling me that they're going to be on duty right through the entire holiday. They won't even have a proper Christmas dinner because they'll still be sifting through the ashes for clues—'

'No dinner?' Maude's social conscience stirred almost visibly. 'On Christmas Day?'

There was an uncomfortable rustle in the room, as though some of them had sensed and disapproved of the direction Maude's hospitable instincts were taking.

'Well, I suppose they'll have something to eat late at night, when they get home,' Iris admitted. 'But it won't be a proper Christmas dinner, with all the trimmings—and with their families around them.'

'That isn't right,' Maude frowned. 'We ought to do something about it.'

'If they're on duty—' Eva Manning murmured tentatively.

'Perhaps I could take over a plate of turkey sandwiches,' Iris suggested.

'They might prefer not to be distracted.' With unusual resolve, Eva Manning insisted upon her original point.

'I hate cops,' Patti said flatly. 'Why do anything about them at all?'

'Patti!' Pammi exclaimed in shocked reproof.

'Well, what good are they?' Patti asked. 'They're

just glorified garbage men. They come on the scene after the wreck has happened. They can pick up the pieces—' her voice wavered dangerously—'but they can't put them together again.'

'Patti—' Looking frightened, Pammi tugged at her sister's arm. 'Come on, Patti. I think we ought to be going now.'

'Don't try to drag me away!' Patti shook off the restraining hand. 'I mean it!'

'Patti, please—'

'*Our* police are different.' Maude rallied to the defence. 'They—'

'Oh, sure, we've all heard,' Patti mocked. '*Your* police are wonderful.'

'Our police,' Maude continued firmly, 'exist to protect society and *we* are society. It's our duty to back them, just as much as it's their duty to protect us. Perhaps we aren't able to "have a go" in some dramatic situation like a holdup, but we can all do our share of backing them in quiet ways, even if that means no more than seeing to their comfort when they're on duty. And I, for one, intend to!'

'Hear, hear!' Iris had not intended to fan the flames of controversy, but Maude had put the case so exactly that she could not hold back.

'I quite agree,' Major Entwistle said, and Eva Manning twittered nervous concurrence.

'They're never around when you want them,' Patti insisted stubbornly. 'Not when there's a genuine emergency. You know that's true.'

'They *are* terribly understaffed, poor dears,' Eva Manning murmured. 'Like the rest of us.'

'Exactly!' Maude glanced involuntarily towards Iris. 'Life is difficult for everyone these days.'

'I hate cops,' Patti muttered stubbornly. 'I hate a lot of people—but I hate cops worst of all.'

'If you object—' Maude began icily. Pushed just that little bit too far, her hospitable instincts were wearing thin under the strain.

'We can worry about all of this tomorrow,' Iris interrupted hastily, before Maude issued an ultimatum she would later regret. 'I have a far more interesting worry at the moment. What do you think? Mr Stein stopped me in the hallway this morning and borrowed three sheets.

'I forgot to tell you—' she apologized hastily to Maude, who had been suitably diverted by this piece of information. 'But I'm telling you now. What on earth do you suppose he wants them for?'

'Did he promise to return them?' Maude went straight to the most urgent point.

'Right after Christmas, he said. But why should he suddenly need all those sheets?'

'The sheets on his bed were changed at the beginning of the week,' Maude said indignantly. 'He shouldn't need any more. Unless something has happened to the ones he already has. You don't suppose—' she voiced the landlady's nightmare—'he was smoking in bed and burned them?

'I don't think so.' Iris shuddered and glanced involuntarily towards the back of the house. 'I don't think anybody is going to be smoking in bed in this neighbourhood for a long, long time to come.'

The chill had crept back into the room. For a short time, the argument had distracted them from the realities of the tragedy that had struck so close to them. An uneasy silenced lengthened.

'Oh, please!' Eva Manning implored. 'This has been such a *pleasant* afternoon—'

'Quite right,' Major Entwistle said. 'No need to spoil it, eh? What's done can't be undone. No sense in brooding over it. Unhealthy.'

The front door slammed and they all seized on the occurrence gratefully.

'Who's that?' Maude demanded, starting for the door.

Iris was closer and opened it and looked out. 'It's Anne,' she reported. 'And Tom.'

'Ask them in,' Maude instructed. 'Everyone else is here. Nearly everyone,' she amended, with a glance around the gathering.

'I've got it!' Patti laughed abruptly. 'Santa Claus— he wants some sacks.'

They looked at her blankly.

'Don't you see?' Under their combined stare, she grew defensive. 'He wants to play Santa Claus—Father Christmas—and he needed them for his sacks. The sheets. Mr Stein—' For a moment, she looked quite erractic. 'Don't you get it?'

'Oh yes, of course.' Eva Manning gave a nervous laugh. 'Yes, you might be right.' It was obvious from her expression that she was not truly amused.

'Ah yes. Jolly good,' Major Entwistle chimed in quickly. His voice was too soothing, his manner too placating.

'Okay.' Patti's eyes narrowed. 'So it wasn't the greatest joke in the world. But, damn it! you don't have to *humour* me!'

'Take it easy, Patti,' Pammi said. 'They're not—'

'You think I don't know?' Patti whirled on her sister. 'They were all right until *you* got here—then they all began to change. What have you been telling them about me?'

'Nothing, Patti.' Pammi began backing away. 'You're just imagining—'

Anne and Tom Imutu walked right into it.

'Don't you dare say a thing like that! Don't you *dare!*' Patti looked as though she might be going to burst into incoherent screams.

'Well, where have you two been all day?' Desperate to avert a scene, Maude swooped on Anne and Tom with unexpected warmth. 'We thought we'd see you long before this.'

'Were we expected?' Tom asked in bewilderment.

'We've been doing some last-minute shopping,' Anne said smoothly. As a long-term resident, she caught the nuances swiftly. The way she carefully ignored Patti proved it. 'And then Tom wanted to book a telephone call to his family in California for Christmas Day and that took quite a lot of time. As it turned out, he'd left it too late, so he'll have to talk to them the day after Boxing Day instead.'

'What a pity,' Maude said. 'The lines get fully booked *so* early. You should have warned him about it.'

'I hadn't realized his intentions, or I would have.'

Tom Imutu laughed abruptly. 'Sorry,' he apologized. 'It was just something I thought of.'

'You ought to share the joke with the rest of us,' Maude said. 'We'd like some light relief ourselves.'

'Maybe tomorrow I will,' Tom Imutu said. He paused and considered. 'Yes, definitely, tomorrow I will,' he promised.

'That's a long time to wait.' Patti had recovered herself. 'We could all use a good laugh right now.'

'Sorry.' Tom Imutu grinned. 'No can do.' He sketched an Oriental shrug of regret. 'Tomorrow.'

'Tomorrow may never come,' Patti said. Perhaps she had been trying for the light touch, but her face shadowed as she heard her own words.

'We were just leaving—' Pammi moved forward and took her sister's arm. 'There's a Carol Service at the church this evening. I thought it would be nice to go.'

'I don't want to go to church!' Patti twisted her arm free.

'Well, *I* do!' For once, it was Pammi's eyes flashing.

Oh.' Patti was taken aback. It was evidently rare for Pammi to make a stand.

'It won't be long,' Pammi coaxed, but there was a trace of steel in her voice. 'And you'll enjoy it once we get there. I know you will.'

Expertly, she was guiding Patti through the door and into the hallway as she spoke.

Iris closed the door thankfully as their voices faded away. She smiled at the others, expecting them to share her relief, but they still seemed caught in the throes of the scene that had been so narrowly avoided.

Only Tom Imutu smiled back.

CHAPTER XXVIII

On the twelfth death of Christmas . . .

Christmas Day in the morning. I wish it weren't.

The church bells began ringing so early, awakening the unbelievers and the agnostics along with the believers. Awakening me from the first unbroken night's sleep I have had in a long time.

Like it or not, we must all be summoned to rejoice on this day of days. I wonder if I could report them to the Noise Abatement Society?

That would teach them a lesson. Not everyone wishes to put up with their nonsense.

And all that discordant clanging has started my head aching again.

Today I *must* take two aspirins—however thoroughly I disapprove of dosing oneself. But there is a long day ahead—and *such* a festive afternoon. I must try to be at my best.

I must get through this day somehow.

How I wish I could simply sleep through it all. Just go to sleep and wake up on the other side of the holiday. After New Year's Day, when the world has come back to its senses again and business is going on as usual.

I always feel much better when I can move about

in the framework of a business day. There is a security in knowing where everyone is supposed to be and what they are supposed to be doing.

Not that they are always doing it.

It would be a simpler world if only people were not so erratic.

Like Iris. One never knows where she is going to be these days. Or what she is going to say.

She ought to be taught a lesson, too.

Where *are* the aspirins? I'm sure I left them here in this drawer. I bought a new bottle just the other day. I *can't* have used them already. But they aren't here now.

The cleaning woman must have taken them. These people are all light-fingered. I'd forbid her the room except that there would be such a fuss about it. Far easier to let the normal routine of the house go on and keep one's valuables in the bank.

Iris comes into all the rooms, too. She claims it's part of her duties as a housekeeper to make certain that the rooms have been properly cleaned and that we have everything we need. But I know the truth about that.

She's snooping!

She needn't think she's fooling *me*. The others may believe her, but they haven't watched her the way I have. I know what she's up to.

I don't like Iris. I don't like any of them.

And yet, I am faced with an entire afternoon and evening in their company. How *could* I have let myself in for such a thing? What could have possessed me?

Hour after hour in that stuffy reception room made

claustrophobic by too many people, too much heat, drink, smoke, noise. Too many strained jokes and forced laughter, too much confusion passing as merriment. Too much of everything.

It would be such a nice house without them all. It was once; it could be again. If only they did not inhabit it.

They've got to go.

Then I could have the whole house to myself. Or, if I wished, find new lodgers. People of the right sort, who'd keep themselves to themselves and not try to intrude on one's privacy. People who, even if I were mad enough to invite them to a Christmas dinner, would never dream of coming.

My sort of people.

But I must not stand here dreaming. Can that clock be right? How long have I been lost in my reverie? I must get dressed. Before someone comes to the door. Such a thing would have been unthinkable once, but the standards in this house have been so lowered that one needs always to be prepared for a knock on the door at any moment.

They'll use the day for an excuse. They believe anything is acceptable on Christmas Day. They'll push themselves in and stare around, all under the guise of good-fellowship and the holiday spirit. I know their game.

But, for today, it is necessary for me to play that game. However much I loathe it. Loathe them.

I must mingle with them today, and smile while doing so. I must join in their stupid games, sing carols, sit around the table with them, pull those ridiculous crackers and wear one of those revolting paper hats, applaud when the blazing plum pudding is carried in . . .

But, first, there will be the turkey.

And, waiting beside the turkey, the carving knife.

The long, sharp, glittering knife . . .

CHAPTER XXIX

O come ye, O come ye . . .

Iris set the last bowl of peanuts on the coffee table and the penultimate plate of canapés on top of the television set. She could hear Maude in the kitchen wrestling with trays of ice cubes, trying to fill the ice bucket for the drinks table. A sudden clattering cascade hit the linoleum and Maude's ferocious mutter was drowned out by running water as she tried to rinse off the ice cubes.

'Never mind,' Iris called out comfortably. 'They say we all have to eat a peck of dirt before we die!'

Judging by the sharpness of her tone, it was probably just as well that Maude's actual words were inaudible over the running water.

Iris smiled, looking around the room, beginning to feel in a party mood. It *had* been a good idea of Maude's, despite all the extra work and preparation. Parties brought people together and it was so much nicer than all of them spending Christmas Day alone in their rooms.

She could hear movement on the upper floors; creaking boards and the restless pacing of people who wanted to be on time for the party but didn't want to be the first to arrive. Soon, however, one of them would make a move and then the others would follow. The party would be in full swing before they realized it.

'I suppose they *are* coming?' Maude appeared in the doorway bearing the ice bucket and obviously in the last stages of Hostess's Nerves.

'If they aren't, we're going to be left with an awful lot of food to eat by ourselves,' Iris said merrily.

'Oh, *don't!*' Maude slammed the ice bucket down on the table, rattling the bottles, and raised a hand to her forehead.

'Oh, Maude!' Iris was instantly sympathetic. '*Not* one of your heads! Today of all days.'

'I don't think so,' Maude rubbed her forehead reflectively. 'It's just tension, I hope. It will go away once the party starts. But I took something, just in case.'

'That should be all right, then. You wouldn't want anything to ruin your lovely Christmas party.'

'If it *is* lovely.' Maude was still disposed towards pessimism. '*Someone* ought to have arrived by now.'

'Why don't you sit down?' Iris suggested. 'You've been working all morning. Relax and let me get you a drink.'

'I can't.' Maude perched on the edge of a chair. 'I ought to baste the turkey again.'

'I'll do it.' Iris thrust a gin and tonic into Maude's unresisting hand and headed for the kitchen.

The deep rich aroma of roasting turkey had permeated every corner of the kitchen accompanied by faint sporadic sizzling noises from the oven. On the table, a large bowl of parboiled potatoes waited to be tipped into the turkey pan and rolled over in the rich juices for the final hour of roasting. Another bowl held crisp green sprouts stripped of their outer leaves, the little cross cut into the base for quicker cooking, ready to be plunged into boiling water at the last moment. Fat sausages lay ready to join the turkey and roast potatoes for the final half-hour's cooking.

An old-fashioned Christmas, Iris thought, with a curious feeling of satisfaction as she stooped and opened the oven door. All the old familiar feeling of comfort and peace and 'God's in his heaven, all's right with the world'. Of course, that was what Christmas was all about.

A gust of hot aromatic air rushed into her face. She pulled the turkey forward and basted it quickly. It *was* fearfully large; she hoped Maude had not underestimated the cooking time needed. It would never do to send their guests away with ptomaine poisoning.

Maude isn't the only one with pre-party nerves. Iris smiled ruefully and shut the oven door. She hoped, with sudden poignant keenness, that it *would* go off all right—for Maude's sake.

They *were* an awfully mixed bag to throw together. So many nationalities, so many different religions. And yet, there was so much good will. Surely that would carry the day, even with such hereditary enemies as Ahmed and Mr Stein.

Nevertheless, she resolved to keep those two as far apart as possible. Not that she expected any real trouble, she simply mistrusted Jacob Stein's impish sense of humour. Whether because he had no sense of humour of his own or because his English was insufficient, poor Ahmed just couldn't cope with it.

She paused in the dining-room, caught by a vague sense of something wrong. Casting an expert eye over the table, she checked for the disquieting factor. The table was all set and waiting. White skeletal stalks of celery nestled between clumps of green and black olives; golden curls of butter nearly matched the gold rims of their dishes; bright fragile wine glasses and gleaming triangles of napkins stood sentinel at every place.

The flowers would probably have to be moved when the food was carried in. The small bouquets on the table could join the big set-piece and bottles of wine on the sideboard. That was all right.

Maude had brought out the best china and silver, glowing against the opulent damask cloth. No second-best for *her* guests, even though they were not the ones she normally entertained.

A large space was already cleared for the turkey platter, with carving knife and fork beside it. Iris smiled wryly. At least, the sight of the carving knife ought to make Ahmed feel at home; it was nearly as long and sharp as a sword. Or did they use scimitars where he came from?

Only the guests were missing. Everything else was ready and waiting.

The knock at the door exploded into the silence. Maude jumped, then laughed nervously as Iris went to answer it.

'We decided we might as well be the ones to push the boat out.' Patti and Pammi crowded into the reception room, laughing. 'Everybody else is just standing around waiting for someone else to go first.'

'Come in,' Maude said unnecessarily, as they were already in. 'What are you drinking?'

'Oh, how delicious it smells!' Pammi sniffed the air rapturously. 'I could put on five pounds by just standing here and inhaling. This is going to be absolutely fatal!'

'It's Christmas,' Maude said. 'No one has a right to worry about their diet on Christmas Day.'

'That's right,' Patti chimed in. 'It's positively antisocial. If you even mention calories, I'll murder you!'

'Well, all right,' Pammi said. 'But if I can't fit that blue skirt when it comes time to leave, you'll have to buy me a new one.'

'It's a deal,' Patti said. 'So long as you leave the blue one behind for me.'

'Then I'll start with some potato chips!' Pammi pounced on them triumphantly.

'Crisps,' Patti corrected.

'Chips!'

'Crisps!'

'Chips! The trouble with you is that you're getting too damned anglicized. They're chips, chips, chips!'

'Girls, girls!' Maude interrupted the amiable bickering. 'Come and tell me what you're going to have to drink.'

There was another knock at the door.

'And hurry up!' Patti pushed Pammi over to the drinks table. 'Here come the ravening hordes—and we were here first. Quick, name your poison or it will be all gone before you can blink.' She and her sister began giggling.

'I seem to have lost my man—' Anne Christopher stood in the doorway with Eva Manning. 'Temporarily, I hope. But Miss Manning was kind enough to say I could come along with her.'

'Lost, strayed but, we hope, not stolen.' Patti turned to greet them.

'Oh, I shouldn't think so.' Anne waved a disclaimer, becoming suddenly very left-handed.

'You never can tell—' Patti wickedly ignored it—'these days.'

'If *I* can't tell—' Anne's left hand danced in the air again—'*no* one can!'

'Hey!' Pammi moved closer, raising a hand in front of her eyes in mock defensiveness. 'Stop waving that thing around—you're blinding me. Diamonds!'

'Well, one, anyway.' Having made her effect, Anne retreated into a modesty which fooled no one. 'Tom got it as a surprise for me. He said he decided a solitaire was nicer than a lot of little ones. And, I must say, I agree.'

'That's right,' Patti grinned. 'As long as you both agree on the *big* decisions in a marriage, the little ones can take care of themselves.'

'Oh!' Belatedly, Eva Manning caught up with the others. 'You're engaged!' She hesitated. 'To that nice—er—*American* boy?'

'That nice *Japanese*-American boy,' Anne agreed. 'He's the only one in my life.'

'And you're going to be *married?* That makes it all right, then.'

'*What* all right?' Anne looked at her blankly.

'Oh!' Realizing what she had said, she stepped back, her face going scarlet. 'I'm sorry. I didn't mean to imply a *moral* judgement—' She broke off, evidently realizing that she was making things worse.

Off to a flying start. Iris winced.

'I'm sorry.' Eva Manning lifted her head and faced Anne squarely. 'I *am* old-fashioned. I can't help it. It's the way we were brought up in my generation.' She looked as though she might be about to cry. 'I'm hopelessly out of date and I can't do anything about it.'

'That's all right,' Annie said swiftly. 'Don't worry. I've heard worse than that—' her mouth twisted briefly—'from my own family.'

So that was why Anne and Tom were spending Christmas in a London lodging-house rather than at home with Anne's family.

'Oh, my dear!' Eva Manning forgot her blunder. 'I *am* sorry.'

'No bones broken.' Anne turned away the unwanted sympathy. She raised her left hand to brush back a lock of hair. 'We'll be living in the States, anyway, as soon as Tom has finished his course here. So it won't make any difference.'

'Drinks!' Maude trumpeted at them. 'Come and get your drinks. I'm not going to stand here all day, you know.'

'Oh yes, I'm sorry!' Eva Manning plunged forward guiltily. 'I didn't mean to keep you waiting. I just—'

'Have you set the date yet?' Iris covered Miss Manning's retreat.

'Early in the New Year, I think.' Anne Christopher grimaced ambiguously. 'I just have a feeling—I've had it for quite a long time now. New Year—new beginnings. It seems right, doesn't it? Tom agrees with me. The sooner, the better, he says.'

'Yes.' Iris was not aware that she sighed faintly. 'I must admit, I'll be glad to see the New Year in. I can't explain why but, somehow, I just have the feeling that *this* year has gone on for far too long.'

'I think everyone feels that about this time of year,' Pammi said. 'Once Christmas is past, I just want to curl up and let the old year tick away and not wake up until a bright and shining New Year's Day. Except—' her face shadowed—'they haven't been so bright and shining for the past couple of years.'

'You're very quiet over here.' Maude appeared behind them, making shooing motions. 'Come along and get your drinks. This is a party—not a wake!'

The others moved away obediently as Iris went to answer a diffident tap at the door. 'Come in, Major.'

Major Entwistle walked into the room stiffly, even more ramrodlike than usual with the frozen horror of a man discovering himself to be the first male arrival at a party full of women. He cast a desperate glance around the room, obviously wishing he could go away and come back later when there were reinforcements.

'Oh, Major Entwistle, I'm so glad you're here.' Maude took in the situation and acted to defuse it. 'Could you take over at the drinks table, please? I must get back to the kitchen and see to the potatoes.'

'Of course. Certainly.' Given a role, Major Entwistle moved forward with assurance. 'Delighted to,' he added in tones of genuine relief.

With an encouraging smile, Iris went over and let him pour her another drink, lest he bolt if he had time to think it over. Surely the rest of the men would arrive at any minute. But why weren't they here now? It wasn't as though they could be expected to gather together over a drink before braving the party—they hadn't much in common. Tom Imutu, at least, should have come with Anne Christopher.

Eva Manning, looking nearly as rigid as the Major, stood with a strained smile on her face staring into space. One of those curious silences had abruptly descended over the room and Maude could be heard quite clearly clattering about in the kitchen.

Absently, Iris counted heads. Seven, including herself. With three more to come. She realized then the cause of her earlier uneasiness in the dining-room.

Maude had laid the table for twelve.

They had discovered the stiff white envelope just inside the front door when they arrived at the house that morning. It had been lying perilously near the point of origin of the fire, obviously put through the letter slot as the lighted match had been. Was it some kind of booby trap?

'To the Two Policemen On Duty.' Sergeant Preston had read out the name of the addressees just above the address. 'That's us, all right.'

'So it would seem.' Superintendent Knowles stood looking down at the envelope. Neither of them were disposed to pick it up and investigate its contents immediately.

Letter bombs were uppermost in their minds as their eyes met. In reflex action, they looked again at the envelope on the charred floor, automatically scanning it for the tell-tale signs.

It was not at all bulky, it did not seem to conceal more than a single sheet of paper. Nor were there any visible wires or grease marks. The address had not been printed in clumsy block capitals but had been written in a fine copperplate. It had not come through the post, however, but had obviously been delivered by hand some time during the night.

'Looks all right,' Preston judged. 'Think we ought to open it? It's addressed to us, after all.'

'Mmmm.' Knowles nudged it cautiously with the tip of his shoe. There appeared to be nothing underneath it. In any case, there would have been littl time or opportunity for their villain to rig a booby trap during the night. Not that their particular villain worked that way—he operated on impulse.

Like writing an impulse letter to the police investigating the case? He hadn't done so before, but the one constant factor about this character was that he *had* no constancy. Anything was possible.

'Mind the fingerprints.' Knowles stepped back, giving permission, and watched as Preston carefully lifted the envelope by its edges.

It was a slow business, but they were in no hurry. When Preston at last unfolded the single sheet of best quality rag content paper, he snorted with amusement.

'We needn't have been so worried about the finger prints—it's signed.'

'Signed?' Knowles started forward eagerly.

'Relax,' Preston said. 'It isn't a confession.' He stared down at it unbelievingly. 'It appears to be an invitation.'

'Invitation?' Knowles tilted the piece of paper so that he could read it.

' "Realize you are on official duty" . . .' Obligingly, Preston helped by reading out highlights. ' "But Christmas Day . . . just an informal gathering . . . Delighted if you would join us . . ." '

'That's a new one,' Knowles admitted. 'I've never had this happen before.'

'Have you ever been on duty like this on Christmas Day before?' Preston countered.

'There *is* that,' Knowles agreed. 'But . . .' He squinted at the flowing signature. 'Maude Daneson . . . who is she? Have we—?'

'House opposite at the back,' Preston said. 'We

talked to the girl, remember? This one is some sort of relative. Lived in the house most of her life. One of the neighbours we haven't interviewed yet.'

'Drinks at three-thirty.' Knowles studied the invitation. 'Dinner about five. Sounds like a pleasant afternoon.' He began strolling thoughtfully towards the rear of the house.

'We couldn't . . . could we?' Preston followed him. They stopped in what had been the kitchen and stood staring across the adjoining gardens. 'It's pretty odd that she thought we might.'

'Oh, I don't know,' Knowles said. 'A lot of people think that Christmas Day cancels out everything else. Look at all the relatives who can't stand each other for three hundred and sixty-four days of the year and yet travel miles to spend Christmas Day together.'

'Like those stories about the first Christmas in World War One,' Preston recollected. 'They say the troops on both sides stopped the firing and there was a spontaneous truce. Both sides walking back and forth across No-Man's-Land, talking to each other and giving each other cigarettes and little presents—'

'Until the top brass discovered what was going on and set them back to killing each other again.' Knowles knew the story, too. 'But you're right. A lot of people, especially amateur killers, look on this as a sort of day of amnesty.'

The curtains parted abruptly in the house opposite. A grey-haired woman appeared in the window of what was obviously the kitchen and looked across at them stolidly for a moment, then began waving and making incomprehensible gestures at them.

Knowles hesitated, then waved back.

'She could be a nice kind citizen,' Preston said

thoughtfully. 'Just wanting to do her bit to cheer the lot of Our Brave Boys in Blue.' He, too, sketched a half-hearted wave.

The woman made a final gesture and disappeared from the window. The curtains swung back into place.

'Or,' Preston finished, 'she *could* be as crazy as they come.'

'In that case,' Knowles said, 'it might be a good idea to go over there and take a long close look at her.'

CHAPTER XXX

Have yourself a . . .

Maude came back into the room looking suspiciously complacent. Far more so than simply putting the potatoes in to roast warranted. Iris wondered what else she had been up to and began to move towards her.

'What's that?' Patti asked abruptly. The others stopped talking and listened.

A ragged attempt at harmony seemed to be echoing down the stairs and advancing along the hallway. The words were blurred and the tune not immediately apparent.

Iris changed course and threw open the door.

'. . . *Orient are . . .*' The chorus wavered, then gained strength. '*We three kings of Orient are . . .*' There was a pause, a clash of notes and syllables, and then the phrase began again. Their identity appeared to be the only thing they were certain of.

'*We three kings of Orient are . . .*'

Self-conscious but determined, they marched into the room, waving brightly-wrapped parcels.

'So *that's* where the sheets went!' Maude exclaimed.

'Dear lady, gentle hostess—' Jacob Stein led the advance upon her. 'We bring you gold, frankincense and myrrh—' He held out his gift. It gurgled.

'Or reasonable facsimiles,' he finished on a lower key.

Maude led the burst of laughter and Major Entwistle started a round of applause.

Bowing and clutching their sheets more firmly around them, they swaggered across the room. Only Ahmed seemed at home in his improvised drapery. Jacob Stein's was coming adrift at its mooring, and safety-pins glinted shamelessly at strategic points in Tom Imutu's.

'Ah-ha!' Tom Imutu broke ranks as he went past his financée. He swooped on her and swept her up into his arms.

'*My desert is waiting . . .*' he warbled unevenly.

'You're out of character!' Mr Stein tried to call him to order. 'That's the Red Shadow, not the Three Wise Men.'

'Speak for yourself,' Tom Imutu retorted. 'It seems wise enough to me!'

'Please,' Ahmed said. 'You are spoiling the effect.'

'All right, I'm outvoted.' Tom dropped Anne back on her feet and she clung to him laughing. 'She's no featherweight, anyway.' He dodged the mock-blow.

'Don't drop the frankincense,' Jacob Stein ordered. 'Present it to our hostess before you begin carousing.'

'Sorry.' Tom Imutu held his parcel out to Maude with a low bow and straightened, clutching his back and doing a bow-legged wobble back to Anne.

'Oh, thank you.' Maude struggled with the wrapping paper in some confusion, as Jacob Stein and Ahmed approached, also thrusting their presents at her. 'One at a time, please,' she protested, laughing.

'Let's open *all* the presents now!' Patti said spontaneously. 'What are we waiting for?'

Perhaps only Iris noticed that Maude glanced surreptitiously at her watch.

'Fine.' . . . 'Good idea!' . . . 'Why not?' ... The others eddied towards the Christmas tree.

Maude looked up, frowning.

'Quarter past four,' Sergeant Preston said. It had been a grey and gloomy day, not relieved by the atmosphere of the charred shell which had grown more oppressive as the day wore on. Now that the only light was a subdued glow from the hissing portable gas lamps, it was enough to make a strong man shudder, if not weep. 'Think we ought to be getting over there now? We're late.'

'By whose reckoning?' Knowles raised a face pitted with sinister shadows, his eyes glittering at the back of cavernous eye sockets.

'The invitation said half past three.'

'For drinks. But the lady added that dinner would be "about five". I read that as an open invitation.'

'Perhaps,' Preston said dubiously.

'No perhaps about it. The lady understands that we're on duty. As I see it, she's given us the option of coming to drinks and dinner, or just to dinner, depending on our duties.'

'Perhaps.' Preston was still dubious. 'But I think we ought to tell her that we'll be late.'

'That's very polite of you, you've obviously been very well brought up.' Knowles's voice rose sharply. 'What makes you think this is a bloody social occasion? Are you letting all the Christmas stars get in your eyes and blind you? Or are you just thinking of your stomach?'

Preston snapped to attention. 'No, sir,' he said stiffly.

'All right.' Knowles's voice reverted to its normal range. 'Then I'll tell you what we're going to do. We're *not* going to let a possible opponent decide the time we ought to be anywhere. We'll wait and let the party get well started. Let everyone get a bit off-balance, perhaps think we're not coming at all. We'll let them all relax and get a few drinks ahead of us.

'*We'll* choose the time we arrive.'

There was the inevitable Christmas gathering problem: whether to give out all the presents at once and then, when everyone had a pile beside them, to indulge in a great orgy of simultaneous unwrapping; or whether to give the presents out one at a time and wait until each was opened and exclaimed over before giving out the next present to someone different.

At a glance from Maude, Major Entwistle had topped up all the drinks to slide them over the initial awkwardness. He was one of the shyest himself, however, and his glass had steadfastly remained at the same level throughout the afternoon.

Of course, Iris thought, there were some people who did not trust themselves to drink.

And others who weren't supposed to. Not that religious prohibitions were impeding Ahmed in any way. Only the glassy look in his eyes betrayed the fact that he was unaccustomed to alcohol and rapidly approaching his level of tolerance. Iris hoped that he would make it through to dinner; once he got some food into him, he ought to be all right.

Perhaps Maude had the same idea. She was consulting her watch again with a worried frown. She looked up and saw Iris watching her.

'I think it's time to put the sprouts on. No. I'll do

it—' She checked Iris's move towards the kitchen. 'You stay here and see that everything is under control. I'll be right back.'

Under control. What an odd expression for Maude to use. Why shouldn't everything be under control? The party was going with a swing and everyone was mixing quite well. Although dinner was yet to come, the party could be considered a success.

Iris wondered suddenly whether Maude's headache was under control. Maude had not mentioned it again—but she wouldn't, not even if the pain were excruciating. She would struggle through the day somehow and collapse after her guests had departed.

'Iris! Iris! Pay attention!' Jacob Stein had appointed himself Master of the Revels and was holding out a long slim package glittering with tinsel. 'This one is for you.'

'Thank you.' Iris took the parcel and felt pieces of wood roll against each other inside. Pencils? Charcoal sticks?

'Go ahead.' Jacob Stein winked at her. His stage prop crown had slipped down over one ear, giving him a rakish appearance. He tried to act indifferent, but there was no doubt who the present had come from. 'Open it!'

Iris felt her colour rise. All eyes were on her. Belatedly, she remembered how much she had always loathed these moments. Today, there wasn't even the excuse that they were all family surrounding her. Oh, but they meant well. She struggled with wrapping that seemed to consist of a cocoon of Scotch tape underneath the tinsel.

'Oh!' It was worth the struggle. 'A full set of brushes! And sable hair! How did you know?' She'd looked longingly at them in the art supply store, but they were so expensive.

'You should always paint in oils. You're good. You ought to have the best equipment.' Suddenly aware that he was being too serious, he grimaced. 'Naturally, sable hair. Treat me right and with another million or so brushes you can make a coat.' He shrugged. 'Well, maybe a jacket.'

'What are these?' Patti had swooped on the tiny packages Eva Manning had scattered over the branches. 'Give these out next, Mr Stein. Please. I'm dying of curiosity.'

'By special request—' Obligingly, he tumbled the packets into his hands and began reading labels that were nearly as big as the packets themselves. 'Another something for Iris—such a popular young lady! And Pammi, and Anne, and Maude—' Mischievously, he withheld Pattie's present until last.

'The Major . . . and Tom . . .' There was one for each of them. 'And even you, Patti. Are you sure you deserve it?'

'Oh, come on!' Patti snatched it from him, tearing at the wrappings.

'Oh!' Patti's face changed abruptly as she lifted the lid of the small leather box. 'Oh, it's beautiful, Miss Manning, but—' She took out an opal brooch, Victorian, valuable.

'You shouldn't have.' Her voice shook with conviction. 'Really, you shouldn't have.'

The others looked uneasily at their own small parcels, suddenly reluctant to open them. A wave of disquiet swept the room. Whatever small gifts they had chosen for Eva Manning were only too obviously going to be out of all proportion to the gifts she was giving.

'Nonsense!' Eva Manning said with forced gaiety. 'Just little trinkets, keepsakes. Go on, open them!'

With a trapped expression, Major Entwistle fumbled at his package and gazed down with dismay. 'My dear lady, this is much too generous.'

'Don't you like them?' Eva Manning seemed close to tears. 'I'd *so* hoped you would.'

'Oh yes. Yes, they're— They're—' He seemed unable to continue. He lifted a pair of black pearl cufflinks from the jeweller's box and stared at them helplessly. 'Er, just what I needed.'

'And you—' Eva Manning whirled on Iris. 'Do you like yours?'

As though released from a spell, the others began to open their small boxes. Iris was aware of Eva Manning's avid gaze as she opened hers.

'Yes, thank you. It's lovely.' Words were inadequate. She hoped her expression conveyed proper gratitude and not the deep distress she actually felt. The heavy cabochon garnet and seed pearl pendant swung on the end of a long gold chain, too ornate and far too expensive.

She thought with embarrassment of her own presents waiting to be opened. She had done sketches —almost caricatures—of everyone and mounted them in plain pastel mats, ready to be hung, or framed more formally if they wished to go to the expense. It had seemed a clever idea when she was working on them. Everyone liked pictures of themselves and they had all praised her work at various times. She had thought a personal present using her time and talent would be a deft and inexpensive solution to the problem of gift-giving.

Now it just seemed parsimonious.

'Beautiful . . .' 'You shouldn't have . . .' The others were also trying to express their awkward thanks. It looked as though Eva Manning had emptied her jewel box—and had not succeeded in buying gratitude. They would all have been happier and more comfortable with book tokens.

'Really, this is *too* much!' Maude muttered under her breath in vexation, shifting a large amethyst ring from finger to finger, trying to find one it fitted. 'Isn't it just *like* poor Eva Manning to get it all wrong?'

'You shouldn't have—' Pammi echoed her sister, a silver-gilt gate bracelet weighing down her slender wrist.

'Nonsense!' Eva Manning said again. 'I've had those things all my life and seldom worn them. They ought to go to you young people—you can get some use out of them. I have no one to leave them to—' her face shadowed—'and nowhere to wear them now.'

'I hope you've kept *some* of your pretty things for yourself.' Major Entwistle bent over her gravely. 'I'd like to take you to the opera in the New Year. As part of your Christmas present.'

'Why, yes, of course. I kept all my mother's things—I couldn't bear to part with *them*. But how exciting! What are we going to see?'

'Er, anything you wish. The choice is yours.' His hesitation betrayed his unfamiliarity with Covent Garden's scheduled programmes. He had obviously spoken on the spur of the moment, effectively supplementing what he felt to be his own inadequate present to Eva Manning. But what of the rest of them?

'We'll do something else, too,' Patti promised rashly. 'How about—'

'Calm, everybody keep calm.' Jacob Stein cut in over the embarrassed protestations. 'Just wait until you see what Ahmed's giving out. We all get a deed to an oil well!'

Everyone laughed except Ahmed.

'It's getting late,' Maude said, checking her watch again. 'I don't think we ought to wait much longer. Dinner will be ruined. Suppose we eat now and open the rest of the presents after dinner?' It was more of an order than a suggestion, but an excellent one.

Gratefully, they began moving into the dining-room. A long distracting interval, breaking the mood before any more presents were opened, was just what they needed at this point. Something else to think about; food and wine to blunt the realization of their own inadequacies in the face of Eva Manning's lavishness.

Maude, as always, had struck exactly the right note.

I can't stand much more of this! How much longer is it going to go on? Look at them all—*damn* them all!

Damn their laughing, jeering faces! Damn their smug superiority! *Damn them!*

And *her!* look at her standing there. So complacent, so self-righteous, so sure of herself. What right has she to be so sure of herself? Of anyone?

They all think they're so smart, so secure, so *safe* in their own little world. That nothing can ever harm them, that the outside world can never touch them.

They think they have the right to sneer at other people, to patronize them.

Someone ought to teach them a lesson.

But I can't think about that now. *My head.* The aspirins didn't work. Perhaps I didn't take enough of them. My head keeps throbbing and a strange buzzing has started in my ears.

And the light! Those glaring pinpoints striking my eyes, reflected off the silver, the glasses . . . the carving knife. The brightness—sharp as a physical blow—adding to the pain. I must turn my eyes away, close them, even.

I must not look at the carving knife.

What shall I do? I can't excuse myself just as we're all sitting down to the table. And even if I did go away and take more aspirins, it would be some time before they began to take effect. *I must get through this meal somehow.*

Perhaps another drink would help. 'Feeling no pain'—isn't that the expression? It seems to work for some people.

How many have I had already? I don't know. One can't keep track when the glass is refilled constantly. 'Top it up', they kept saying.

I know their game! They'd like to see me drunk and disgracing myself. That would prove *their* superiority. Then they could laugh and jeer all the more. I won't give them the satisfaction!

But I must do something to try to control this raging pain. Perhaps one more glass. Already, beneath the pain, I feel quite pleasantly floating. Another glass—or two—might remove the pain and just leave the floating sensation. That *would* be nice.

'Major Entwistle,' Maude said, for the second time. 'Would you pour the wine, please?'

'Eh?' Major Entwistle had been standing as though in a trance, staring at the table. He lifted his head and looked at Maude vaguely.

'The wine,' Maude prompted patiently. 'Before you sit down, would you pour the wine, please?'

'Oh, of course. Of course.' Recalled to duty, Major Entwistle took one of the tall bottles from the sideboard and began filling glasses.

He had been a million miles away, Iris thought. Probably they all were, or at least one small part of them was. It was inevitable today. Memories of other Christmases would tug at them all day, fading and returning again as some familiar aspect of the traditional observance tipped them back into the world they had known in their yesterdays.

'Look! Crackers!' Mr Stein broke the spell, snatching up the bright red and gold object beside his plate and flourishing it. 'Everybody pull!'

Little explosions resounded around the table as they turned to their partners and tugged at the snaps.

The smiles of Patti and Pammi were a shade too bright and they did not quite meet each other's eyes as they became over-busy extracting the paper hats and smoothing out the mottoes. The tiny favours fell unnoticed to the tablecloth.

Both Ahmed and Eva Manning nearly upset their wine in the confusion of dealing with what—to Ahmed, at least—were unfamiliar objects.

Ahmed winced at the noise and reached unsteadily for his glass, leaving Eva to try to carry the Christmas spirit all by herself.

'Just look!' she exclaimed. 'Look, Ahmed, you've

got a sweet little horseshoe. That's supposed to be lucky, you know, a horseshoe . . .'

His eyes, glazed with incomprehension, met her own. She shuddered visibly and tried again.

'*So* clever of Maude to have remembered *all* the trimmings, don't you think?' Too late, the realization obviously came to her that Ahmed had no idea of what 'trimmings' were—perhaps not even what Christmas was. She smiled at him over-brightly and reached for her own glass.

'Perhaps—' Maude hovered in the doorway—'perhaps, you'd be kind enough to carry in the turkey for us, Major Entwistle? It *is* rather heavy—'

'Of course, of course.' Obligingly, Major Entwistle sprang forward.

'Here, I say—' Jacob Stein looked around the table. 'We aren't all here yet, are we?' He looked pointedly at the two empty places at the foot of the table. 'There seem to be a couple of us missing.'

'No one is missing,' Maude said coldly. She glanced at her watch and at the empty places. 'I'm afraid I . . . miscalculated. We're all here, Mr Stein.'

'Oh.' Abashed, he cast about for a diversion. 'Here!' He picked up the paper hat that had fallen from his cracker and shook it out with distaste. 'I'm not having this! I refuse to be demoted!'

One saw his point. The limp paper circle punctuated by half-hearted peaks would make a poor substitute for the glittering foil crown already on his head.

'What do you say?' He looked at his fellow-Royals.

'Right!' Tom Imutu tossed his paper hat aside. 'They can't do that to us. We'll stand pat on the hand we already have. Won't we, Ahmed?'

Hearing his name, Ahmed turned and blinked

vaguely in the general direction of the authoritative voice.

'Our colleague agrees,' Tom Imutu translated blithely. 'Away with inferior trappings of royalty!' He picked up the paper crown again and tossed it farther away from him. It was well that Maude had not yet lit the candles in the centre of the table.

Ahmed blinked, then followed suit.

'Not there,' Maude said briskly. 'Leave space for the turkey.' Major Entwistle appeared in the doorway, carrying the heavily-laden platter.

'Just there, please, Major,' Maude directed. 'Right by the carving knife and fork. Iris, if you'd help me—'

Iris began ferrying in the potatoes and sprouts, gravy boat and bread sauce, while Maude directed the placement of each dish and saw to it that the Major refilled all the glasses again.

At last everything was arranged to Maude's satisfaction and she looked around the table with a small sigh of accomplishment.

'Now then, Major Entwistle,' she said. 'Would you like to carve?'

The air was minimally warmer outside than it had been within the gutted house, which was not saying much. The sky was black with the threat of rain, or possibly hail. The lights of the house across the way looked bright and festive, promising warmth, food, drink and comfort, if not pleasant companionship. You couldn't have everything.

'Think it's about time for us to go over?' Preston asked hopefully. 'They ought to be fairly mellowed by now.'

'They ought,' Knowles agreed.

'Do we use the front door or the back?' The invitation had mentioned that the back door would be left on the latch for them, but if Knowles wanted to throw anyone off-balance it might be better to go round to the front door and ring the bell. It would give just the slight reminder that this might be an official call, after all.

'Good question.' Knowles stepped out on to the seared grass. 'What do you think?'

A sudden scream cut through the reflective silence, then another. High-pitched screams of terror emanating from more than one throat inside the brightly-lit house.

'Come on!' They sprinted for the hole in the fence.

As they reached it, the screaming stopped abruptly. The sudden silence was worse than the screaming had been.

'It's been a long time,' Major Entwistle demurred. 'I'm not sure I can remember the knack—' He reached for the carving knife.

Eva Manning snatched it up a split second ahead of him.

Major Entwistle looked with disbelief at the long thin slash across the palm of his hand. Even as he pulled his hand back, the blood welled up and began dripping across the shining white tablecloth.

'No! Noooo!' An eardrum-shattering scream came from Patti, echoed immediately by Pammi.

Ahmed turned hazily and fell back against his chair, one hand rising incredulously to cover the deep gash that had appeared across his throat.

'Tom, don't!' Anne clutched at Tom Imutu as he tried to get up. 'She's insane! That knife—'

'She's gone mad!' Maude's voice rose sharply. 'Utterly mad!'

'Don't call me that!' Eva Manning backed away from the table, the knife held in front of her.

Patti and Pammi stopped screaming abruptly, sensing the danger in calling attention to themselves in any way.

Major Entwistle, his face blank with shock, abstractedly picked up his napkin and wound it around his injured hand.

Ahmed lay back in his chair, his eyes following the trail of his own blood as it rolled down the sheet twisted around his shoulders.

They stared at Eva Manning, waiting, not daring to make a sudden move for fear of setting her off again.

It was impossible, Iris thought. Things like this didn't happen to people one knew, in well-ordered homes. And yet, those *were* the sort of people things happened to, the places where they happened. One read about it in the papers every day. *The papers—*

'Oh God!' Iris whispered. 'Those other people. All around us and coming closer. And the fire—'

'You!' Eva Manning whirled and began advancing on Iris. 'I know all about *you!* Spying! Lying about me!'

'No, Miss Manning—' Iris tried to push back her chair, but she was wedged in by Jacob Stein on one side and Pammi on the other, both as paralysed by horror as she was. She could not get away. 'Please—' She stared helplessly at the sharp point of the knife, coming closer.

'You first,' Eva Manning said. 'Then I'll settle with the others.' She advanced steadily, eyes glittering, lost in some private deadly world of her own. Abruptly, she began singing in a high reedy voice.

'*On the first death of Christmas . . .*'

Iris was aware of blurred shadows moving in the kitchen doorway, but could not raise her eyes from the knife. It was as though she felt she could control it in some way by her gaze; if she looked away for an instant she would immediately feel the sharp bite of the blade and—

Everything happened at once. Maude hurled the gravy boat. Jacob Stein hurled his chair over backwards, crashing to the floor, but deflecting Eva Manning's aim. The police rushed forward to seize her.

The others broke free of the table and rushed to help the police overpower Eva Manning. The struggle was brief and fierce, but ended when she collapsed abruptly, the knife falling from her hand as she struck the floor.

In the sudden lull, Jacob Stein struggled to his feet, clutching his back.

'Maude—' he shook his head in awe. 'Never let it be said that you don't throw a wild party!'

CHAPTER XXXI

Should auld acquaintance be forgot . . .

By quarter to twelve, they had all found themselves gathered into Maude's flat. Anne and Tom had been the last to arrive and Maude had intercepted them before they reached the stairs. They did not appear surprised.

'We were out to dinner and suddenly I couldn't bear to stay in that restaurant any longer,' Anne explained. 'Not to see the New Year in. It didn't seem right. It seemed as though we should be back here instead.'

'We felt that, too,' Patti said. 'Pammi's flying back to Toronto tomorrow and we'd been out, too, having a private farewell. Only then, it didn't seem right to keep to ourselves. We've all—' she waved a hand around the room—'been through so much together. Lifetimes in just a few hours. It seemed as though we all ought to be together to see the Old Year out—'

'And the New Year in,' Maude said firmly. 'A *Happy* New Year.' Her tone defied it to be anything else.

'It could hardly be much worse,' Iris said quietly. It was still difficult to believe that the Christmas party and the past few days had actually happened. But the bandages on Ahmed and the Major were all too vivid reminders that they had. And Mr Stein, sitting stiffly upright, was another—his physiotherapist had promised him that he would be as well as ever, give or take another six months.

'To *think* that she was doing all those terrible things—' Patti shuddered. 'And then coming back to *this* house and none of us ever suspected.'

'Yes.' Maude was tight-lipped. It was, after all, *her* house.

'She didn't suspect it herself,' Mr Stein said. 'Perhaps that's the worst part of all.'

'It's as well that she never regained consciousness,' Major Entwistle said. 'She never could have lived with herself if the operation had been successful and she'd been forced to realize that she'd been responsible for all those terrible murders—'

'Not *responsible*,' Maude corrected. 'She may have committed them, but she wasn't really responsible.'

'That song she was singing,' Patti said. 'It was "The Twelve Days of Christmas", wasn't it? Only her mind turned it into "Deaths". She was going to kill us all, if she hadn't been stopped. And she *did* kill twelve—if you count herself—when they totalled it all up—'

'I don't think we should dwell on it,' Mr Stein said. The media had hashed it over enough. 'Let's make it the New Year's resolution for all of us that we won't talk about it any more.'

'But it was all so awful,' Pammi said. 'And Patti and I feel so strange about that expensive jewellery she gave us just before the last. Do you think we ought to turn it back to her estate? Who inherits, anyhow?'

'I believe there's a cousin somewhere,' Maude said.

'Very distant—I'm not sure they ever met. We were more a part of her life than her relatives.'

'Exactly.' Major Entwistle stared down thoughtfully at the black pearls gleaming in his cuffs. 'She wanted *us* to have those things. I believe that might have been the last gesture of the *real* Eva Manning before the tumour destroying her brain turned her into the final monster.'

'Poor woman,' Ahmed croaked. His throat would give him difficulty for some time yet.

'When you put it like that,' Patti said, 'then we can't give the things back, can we? It would be like turning our backs on her. And she *was* nice—when she was herself.'

'Probably we'll wear it some day,' Pammi said. Reality shadowed her face. 'Probably we'll even make a talking point of it when it's far enough into the future. Anyway, it will sure make a story to tell our grandchildren.'

The clock began to chime twelve, as though tolling once for each victim—including Eva Manning.

'Midnight,' Maude said.

'So the old year is finally over,' Anne Christopher said softly. She reached for Tom Imutu's hand.

They all raised their glasses and there was a commemorative pause, as though no one wanted to be the first to propose the toast. Then they all spoke at once.

'Happy New Year!'